The Dream of a Cowboy

Crossroads Creek Cowboys - Book 5

Elsie Davis

Sweet Romance Publishing

Sweet Romance Publishing

Sweetromancepublishing.com

PO Box 778

Liberty, NC 27298

Ephesians 4:32
"Be kind and compassionate to one another, forgiving each other, just as in Christ God forgave you."

Chapter One

♥

"**I**'VE GIVEN PEANUT AN antibiotic and I put some salve on her cut. Monitor the dog to make sure she doesn't show signs of infection over the next few days," Joe said, packing up his medical bag.

"Thanks for coming out on such short notice, Dr. Granger. My daughter would lose her mind if anything happened to her faithful canine friend. With Dr. Holcomb on vacation and the next regular vet over in Wylie, you were the first person I thought of. I still can't imagine what possessed the beagle to sneak under the fence into the bullpen," Bill Riley said, stroking his bearded chin.

"Curiosity for sure, but hopefully, a lesson learned. Beagles aren't exactly a good match on a ranch." Joe grinned and shook his head. They'd had this discussion once before, but a pet was a pet no matter where you lived.

"Tell me about it. And if anyone had asked me first, I would have said no and steered them toward a Collie or something more useful to help me with the cattle," Bill said.

Joe started for the door, knowing time was limited. Things would be behind for the rest of the day after this emergency call, but then, it would seem like most days were like this. "Maybe it will work out. I've got to run and grab some supper before my next appointment."

"You work too hard. Felt bad calling you, but I didn't know what else to do." Bill followed him out to the porch.

"Calling me was the right thing. And yes, it's been tough trying to meet demand since Dr. Walters retired from our business, but I do my best. Look at the bright side...non-stop appointments leave me little time for anything else, including boredom." Joe grinned, not wanting Bill to feel guilty for adding to the workload.

"There is that. Why don't you hire someone or get an intern from Dallas University?" Bill asked.

It was the same thing he got asked over and over, and the answer was always the same. "You know me. I like the personal, small-town approach. It's why I bought the business from Dr. Walters in the first place instead of going some fancy city route. Crossroads Creek is my home and always will be."

"I get that, but you can't run the business alone. Call Ralph at the university and let him find you someone to help."

"I'm just not sure if an intern will care as much as I require, and my reputation as the local vet means a lot to me. My clients are the top priority." It had been so much easier before Perry retired, and perhaps one day, change would be inevitable. Next year, he'd look into it, but this year, the extra income went a long way to paying the bank on the loan he took out to buy Perry outright.

"An admiral trait and one the whole town loves, but if you run yourself ragged, we all lose."

A valid point for sure. "I'm good for now. It helps me keep a pulse on the community."

"More like in control." Bill chuckled.

"That too. Later," he said, waving as he headed for his black Chevy Silverado. Tossing the bag in the open compartment box, he closed the lid and locked it. The second he slid into the driver's seat, his stomach growled, signaling it was past dinner time. He would have to cut his dinner hour to thirty minutes, but luckily, his next appointment wasn't of the animal variety. Instead, his meeting was with Perry to straighten out some paperwork issue the bank needed corrected pertaining to the sale of the business.

Pulling off the main road, he went slowly so as not to kick up a ton of dust on the truck, not relishing the idea of adding truck wash to his to-do list. It was always the hazard of a gravel road and living in the country, but he wouldn't have it any other way.

More than ready for a break, he was disappointed to see a car parked in front of his home. Probably a client with a sick animal that desperately needed attention, and they didn't bother to call. His door was open 24/7. *Literally*. He would never turn anyone away, his heart as big as Texas for the animals he treated. It was why he became a vet.

Joe slid out of the truck and approached the porch, surprised to see a young woman and her daughter...but no animal on a leash, or in a lap, or in a box, for that matter. In fact, a second sweep of the area revealed no animal at all. He frowned, wondering what they were selling. Or maybe the little girl was doing a fundraiser for school. Letting loose a heavy sigh, he resigned himself that dinner would have to wait a few more minutes. "Good evening. How can I help you?" he asked, drawing near.

The woman jumped to her feet, her purse dropping on the porch. She had been intent on her phone and must not have heard him arrive. The top of her head only reached about shoulder high on him. Her slender figure, vibrant sea-blue eyes, and short blonde hair more than caught his attention. She seemed vaguely familiar, but Joe couldn't figure out why...and he knew everyone from Crossroads Creek, or close to everyone. Which meant she wasn't from around here.

He held out his hand when she didn't speak. "What can I help you with, Ms...." he drawled, asking again and wondering why she was looking at him as though she'd seen a ghost, her pale face void of color.

She shook his hand. "My name's Marissa. And you're Dr. Granger...J...Joe Granger." There was no question in the statement, as though she knew the answer. There wasn't a hint of a smile pinching at her cheeks. Clearly, this wasn't a happy visit.

"I am. Do you have an animal that needs tending?" he asked, looking more closely at the young girl who had moved close to Marissa. Eyes the color of chocolate brown accented by thick brows stared back at him. The freckle-faced girl with her shimmering blonde sun-kissed hair, was a stark reminder of his ex-wife. Joe closed his eyes, stepping back to regroup. He didn't know what was going on, but it spelled trouble. Little tiny pricks of warning bells were going off.

"No animal. This is a personal visit, and you and I need to talk," Marissa said, her voice gaining confidence.

"What did you say your last name is?" Joe asked, one piece of the puzzle falling into place.

"I didn't. It's Marissa Johnson." She brushed her hair back off her face and stared back at him.

"I see. I'm guessing you're Molly's sister then?" The two sisters were both blonde and short, but that's where the similarity ended.

Marissa had been the sweet and shy version of his outgoing, need to be the center of attention, ex-wife.

"I am," Marissa nodded, a flash of pain in her eyes.

"There's not much to talk about then, as that's a past I prefer not to discuss. Living it was enough to last me a lifetime. What does she need? Money? I'm fresh out," he added coldly, his mood shifting with lightning speed. A fundraising request would have been preferable to this.

Marissa shook her head, her lips pursed. "It's not that easy. You need to hear me out...please," she added, almost as an afterthought.

Joe checked his watch. "Fine. So talk, I'm listening. This needs to be quick. I've got to eat dinner and be at a meeting in twenty minutes."

Marissa's eyes darted in the young girl's direction and then back at him. "We should talk privately."

"Fine. We can go into the house, but you've got ten minutes, so talk fast."

"Delia, why don't you get your soccer ball from the car and practice in the yard? I'll be watching from the window inside the house."

The young girl suddenly smiled. "Okay, Aunt Marissa. Is this the man you wanted to see?"

"It is, darling."

Aunt Marissa.

Not mom.

Molly's daughter? *Not his problem, not by a long shot.* The wife and family he once dreamed of having was a thing of the past. Molly had seen to that with her cheating ways. After Joe divorced her, the idea of ever trusting another woman in his life was a mistake he wasn't willing to repeat. *Once was more than enough.*

The young girl got her soccer ball from the car and started kicking it in the air, bouncing it off her sneakers. It was quite an impressive move, but Joe forced himself to return his attention to Marissa. "Shall we? You're down to eight minutes and counting," he said, holding the screen door open for her to pass inside.

They moved into the living room, and Joe flung his cowboy hat on the sofa, turned, and waited for Marissa to speak. She moved to the front window to watch her niece. Marissa's fingers gripped the back of the chair, the pressure turning them white.

"What's so important you needed to talk to me privately? Molly and I haven't been together in eight years, so—"

"She's your daughter. Delia, that is...is your daughter. I had to find you and let you know. I'm so sorry," she added in a sudden rush.

Joe laughed. "You've got this all wrong. I don't have a daughter. Molly signed the divorce papers and a statement that she wasn't pregnant. Try the guy who came after me...the hot shot car driver she ran off to the Carolinas with," he said, unable to keep the disdain out of his voice. Whatever game Molly and her younger sister were playing ended right here and now.

Marissa shook her head. "Molly lied."

Joe gripped the back of the sofa, his bloodless fingers a match to Marissa's at this point. "No way. Is this some scheme to get money? I'm not an idiot and I know how these things work. You can't march in here with your sister's kid and tell me I'm a daddy, and then what? *Write a check, please.* I won't do anything of the sort unless there's a paternity test done. So perhaps you should go back to wherever it is you came from and try someone else." This was total insanity and nothing he had time to deal with. His day had taken a decidedly worse turn.

"Dallas," Marissa said, her gaze landing on him.

Joe frowned, not following the conversation. But then, how did one follow anything when being charged with having fathered a child eight years ago? "What?" he asked, trying to regroup.

"Dallas is where I came from...and I understand this must be a complete shock, but Delia's your daughter. I'm just the messenger."

Joe flopped down on the sofa, running both hands through his hair. Why was Marissa sticking to the claim he was the father? They were words he had longed to hear when he was married to Molly. Though back then, the plan was for the traditional route. Married. Then pregnant. Then he and his wife at the hospital, holding their new bundle of joy.

But this...the girl had to be seven or eight, and it was the first he knew of her existence. Not that he believed for one minute Delia was his daughter. Molly hadn't been faithful, so there was no way to know for sure without a paternity test. Images of Molly begging him to forgive her and not file for divorce, filled his brain. What she hadn't counted on, though, was that he would have never stayed in a loveless marriage with an adulterous woman. His faith and his pride wouldn't let him.

Was it even remotely possible Marissa was telling the truth? Joe stood and moved to stand near Marissa, wanting to get a good look at Delia. The problem was, Molly not telling Joe would have been her way to pay him back for his decision to leave. Payback was something she'd perfected over the years. But this, this was way beyond anything he thought she was capable of. And why hadn't she come in person to deliver her bombshell?

Joe couldn't get sucked into the illusion that he was suddenly a father. "Why are you here and telling me this now? Where's Molly?"

Marissa's eyes were glassy, and she brushed the tears off her cheek. "Molly was killed in a car accident on the Autobahn while vacationing in Germany. I'm Delia's guardian, but a long time ago, Molly let slip something about you being Delia's father. I didn't believe her, but I was recently going through some of her papers and found Delia's birth certificate. It names you as the father."

Joe sucked in a deep breath. This was wrong on so many levels. The fact Molly was dead drained him further of emotion. It wasn't something he would have wished on her, no matter what she had done to him. This wasn't the time to think about Molly...not with Marissa claiming Delia was his daughter. "That still doesn't mean she's mine. Molly's deceit clearly held no bounds."

Marissa placed a hand on his arm, willing him to listen. "You have every right to think what you're thinking, but I believe this is true. I'm here because it's the right thing and I want to right Molly's wrong. As Delia's legal guardian, I felt it was in the child's best interest to meet her father. She's been through so much, and more love and support would be the best thing for her after losing her mom."

A daughter. His appetite vanished and, in its place, questions that couldn't be readily answered. Joe continued to watch Delia as she played ball. *His daughter.*

Maybe.

Hopefully.

Not that he knew the first thing about kids or parenting.

Joe's phone rang, and he glanced down at the screen. "Sorry, I've got to run. I'm late for my meeting with Dr. Walters," he said, reminding Marissa he didn't have time to hash this out.

"Be right there," he told Perry. "Yes, I got caught up with something at the house. I'm headed out the door now."

Joe hung up and pocketed the phone. "Look, I've got an appointment in town. It won't take long, and clearly, we need to talk about this more. Will you stay for the night?"

"I don't know. I could get something in town, I suppose," Marissa said, not sounding entirely sure of a change in her plans.

"There's only one bed-and-breakfast and the Hot August Nights festival is going on. The place will be booked solid. I've got two extra bedrooms in the main house you can use. I'll stay in the bunkhouse, and you can have the run of the place," he added to relieve her worries.

Marissa brushed her hair away from her face, the nervous gesture more than a little telling. "Please stay," he said, sensing her indecision.

Marissa nodded. "I guess we can stay one night. You and I can talk more when you get home and after Delia's gone to bed."

"Thanks. Works for me." Joe paused at the front door. "Get settled in the two rooms across from each other down the hall. You can share the bathroom. Eat what you want, and I'll be right back."

Marissa nodded, though her expression said she wasn't happy about the delay.

Chapter Two

♥

JOE DROVE TO THE Golden Spoon, where he was to meet Perry. The last forty-five minutes of his life had been a blur of emotions and turmoil all rolled into one. *A daughter*. It didn't seem possible. For so long, he'd wanted a family and now it would seem he had one. If Marissa was to be believed, that is. Actually, it came down to whether Molly told the truth. Something he couldn't bank on.

Except, if it was true, it would change his life entirely. Not that it would be a bad thing, just huge. In fact, it would be marvelous, but he dared not get his hopes up too high, only to have the dream snatched away yet a second time.

Though seeing as he just bought the veterinary practice, he wasn't sure how he could fit anything else into the schedule, much less a child. Everything hinged on the if, because if Delia was his daughter, he would move heaven and earth to have her in his life.

And not just part-time.

Joe parked the truck and headed inside, where he spotted Perry in a corner booth. "Sorry I'm running late. Got caught up at the house with some things, and didn't even have time to eat. I'm starved," he said, sliding into the open side.

Perry chuckled. "It's a never-ending cycle, but don't say I didn't warn you." He pushed a plate of French fries in Joe's direction.

"How did you manage it all?" Joe asked, snagging a few. Fast food wasn't his normal meal of choice, but at least these were baked and not fried. He had to be careful what he ate after being diagnosed with Celiac disease years ago.

"I hired you as an intern, promoted you to manager, and then sold half the business to you. Crossroads Creek isn't a huge place, but the animals outnumber the people."

"Good point. Crazy, but true." He helped himself to a few more French fries, something to tide him over until he got back to the house. But then what? Two house guests were waiting on his return, and Joe didn't have a clue how this would work out.

"So, what was it this time? A mare giving birth...or a chicken gone broody?" Perry asked after wiping his mouth clean of the ketchup that had slipped out of the hamburger and onto his chin.

"Neither. Try a daughter on the doorstep." No sense delaying the conversation, and any advice would be welcome.

Perry's confused expression echoed his own internal dilemma. "What's that supposed to mean? Whose daughter showed up at your place?"

"My daughter, or so I'm told. Do you remember Molly?" Joe asked.

Perry's brow suddenly rippled with deep grooves. "Of course, how could I forget?" he said, disdain evident in his voice.

"Well, her sister, Marissa, was waiting on my porch when I stopped by the house this evening. She claims the young girl she brought with her is Molly's daughter. More specifically, *my* daughter. One Molly never mentioned, and if you recall, also signed a statement for the divorce that she wasn't pregnant." Just thinking about it now had the power to make him seethe with anger.

Perry shook his head, one hand rubbing the back of his neck. "Oh, boy."

"No, oh, girl. Her name is Delia." Joe smiled at the irony of it all for the first time. None of this made sense, but then, if Molly lied, why would he be surprised? Their marriage was a lie, so why not the rest of her life?

"Quite the bomb. No wonder you were late and seemed stressed. What are you going to do about it? What does the sister want? And where's Molly in all this?" Perry fired off the questions, still shaking his head as he tried to catch up on the developing situation.

The older man started off as his mentor and had become a close friend. Joe valued his opinion above all others and was hoping he had plenty to give. "Molly died in a car accident over in Germany. Marissa claims her sister once hinted that I was the father of her child, but never confirmed it. Then Marissa found a birth certificate in Molly's belongings with my name on it. She said it was only right that I was told the truth. Except we both know a name on a birth certificate proves nothing."

"Is there a chance the girl's yours?"

Joe shrugged. "I don't know, maybe. She looks a lot like Molly, but her eyes look like mine. And her nose, for that matter." Joe recalled the sweet-faced girl staring up at him, a questioning look in their warm chocolaty depths. "The only thing I know for sure is that if she is my daughter, I'll want full custody.

Marissa misjudged me if she thought otherwise."

"You're not exactly in a place to suddenly start taking care of a child. You've been divorced for almost eight years. So, what is this girl...about sevenish?"

"Yes, on both counts. I agree, but Delia would be my family. A daughter I didn't get to spend time with for the past seven years. Nothing else would be more important than her and making up for lost time. It's not a quick process to find out the legitimacy of the claim. What I really need is help with my appointments, now more than ever. I'll text Ralph and see if he has a Dallas University graduate willing to come out for an interview tomorrow on such short notice. There should be someone looking to complete an internship requirement. There's simply no other choice with this new development." There was so much to consider, but the business took a back burner to family. And not just any family...a daughter.

"Good idea. Just be sure to give the intern a chance...the same way I did with you."

Joe shook his head. "You gave me a chance because I grew up here. I don't know of any locals enrolled at the school looking to get stuck in the middle of nowhere, Texas. Most of the graduates are looking to be a small animal vet in a big city job."

"You're probably right, but you might be pleasantly surprised. You should also plan to get a paternity test right away. You never know the angle people might have when they spring up out of nowhere with a child in tow that they are claiming is yours."

Christina stopped by the table. "Just checking in to see if either of you need anything. Tonight's special is roast beef with gravy and potato, Joe, if you're interested."

"A water would be good, but nothing else. Thanks," Joe said. The roast beef sounded good and was tempting but not with Marissa and Delia back at his place waiting on him to return.

"I'm good, and you can bring my tab," Perry added.

"No worries." Christina picked up the mostly empty dinner plate, leaving the basket of fries for them to nibble on.

"I know a paternity test is the only real way to know for sure," Joe said, lowering his voice so as not to be overheard. "But my heart goes out to the child either way. I mean, what if she knows that's why they're here and then it turns out to be a tremendous disappointment?"

"It's hard to say, but I reckon you might be right. The girl is old enough to reason some things out for herself. But better to find out the truth quickly, rather than drag this out. Where are they staying in the meantime?"

Joe let out a heavy sigh. "My place."

"What? That seems a bit unorthodox."

"I had to leave to meet you, and I needed time to talk to Marissa. It was easier this way. I'd like her to stay longer, if I can convince her.

I'll know more after I've heard what Marissa has to say."

Perry frowned. "I don't know about this, Joe. Sounds to me like someone's trying to pull the wool over your eyes."

"I understand all that...but what if Delia is my daughter? I'm not willing to take the chance and let Marissa waltz out of Crossroads Creek with her until I know for sure. I can't help but be angry at all the time I've lost with Delia if it turns out she really is my daughter. Baby moments. First steps. First foods. First words. First everything. It's so wrong on every level and I won't lose another second of watching her grow up." His offer had been born of desperation, but it was the only leverage he had to keep Delia close at hand.

"I'm truly sorry and understand where you're coming from. Just be careful. Pray about it and God will guide you in the right direction," Perry said, pulling an envelope out of his shirt pocket and sliding it across the table. "I've got to run. This is the new corrected deed I need you to sign. This is what they changed." Perry pointed to the revised seller entity. "Just take this to the bank and have someone notarize it, and they can get it back to Jarod to have the deed re-recorded."

"I'm just glad they figured it out. I've got to get back to the house and check on my houseguests."

"Not sure how the mistake was made, but this will fix everything to put the business entirely in your name. It's good that you could squeeze in some time to meet up with me. It's always good to see you and catch up. Though this time, there's way more going on." Perry chuckled, his toothy grin setting Joe at ease.

It was a good reminder not to get so caught up in the drama of the situation and to remain grounded. Level-headedness would always prevail. "It's fine. I still wish you would get bored, change your mind, and come back to work." Joe laughed.

Perry shook his head and grinned. "Not a chance. Started dating the sweetest woman over in Wylie. Who knows, maybe love can find an old fool."

"Good for you."

Joe's phone rang. "Hello, Dr. Granger."

"Hey, Joe, it's Chad. I'm so glad you answered. I've got a heifer struggling with the birth of her calf. What do I do? She's getting tired and nothing's happening." Chad Thompson lived on the outskirts of town, running a herd of dairy cattle. If he was calling for help, there was a serious problem.

"I'm on my way." He pushed the end button and slid the phone into his pocket. "Duty calls."

"Better you, than me." Perry grinned.

Joe hurried out, backing out of the parking spot and headed down Main Street. He reached for his phone to call Marissa and let her know about the change in plans until he realized he never got her phone number. This might be a long night, and hopefully, she would understand.

Chapter Three

♥

MARISSA'S STOMACH RUMBLED. THERE hadn't been much in Joe's cupboards for dinner that would make a quick meal, so she was still hungry. The tomato soup was good, but not filling. Luckily, she'd found a bag of apples, and a small portion of frozen tater tots to add to the mix.

She closed the book she'd been reading and looked up at her niece. "It's getting late, sweetheart, and it's time for bed."

Delia yawned. "I am sleepy. Goodnight, Aunt Marissa."

"Give me a second to clean up the dishes while you brush your teeth and then I'll tuck you. I know this is a strange place and don't want you to be uncomfortable."

"I'm a big girl and you already showed me my room," Delia said, heading down the hall. "I like that we're staying here. Mr. Granger has a big yard to play in and I want to check out the barn. I wonder if he has animals in there?"

"I don't know, but I doubt we'll be staying long enough for you to explore. Thanks for being okay with the change in plans to stick around for the night."

Delia shrugged. "Maybe I'll get up extra early to check out the barn. This place is so much bigger than where we live in Dallas."

"That's because so many people live in the city and there's only so much space for everyone to live. Both the city and the country have pros and cons," Marissa said, defending her decision to live in the city. Not that she needed to, but the words spilled out anyway.

"Goodnight," Delia said, skipping off down the hallway and out of sight.

Her niece was growing up too fast, and Marissa wanted to hang on to her sweet innocence for as long as she could. The teen years would be here all too quickly. "Good night, Delia," she said in a low voice, knowing she wouldn't be heard.

While Marissa waited for Joe to come back from his appointment, the thought of driving off into the sunset had crossed her mind. *Repeatedly.*

Instead, she waited, the conversation replaying in her head. Maybe she could have eased into the daughter part of things better, but was there really any good way to tell a guy he was a dad? And that the mom, in some twisted way, wanted to hurt him and keep him in the dark? Joe had seven years without his daughter. No wonder he was having a difficult time believing. Coming here was the right thing to do, not that she hadn't prayed for a different answer. What if Joe tried to take Delia away? Did a natural father have more rights than a legal guardian? She didn't think so, given the situation. It was always what was best for the child...and that was Marissa. After all, she'd practically raised Delia from infancy whenever her sister wanted to run off and play.

In her heart, the truth always stared back at her in the mirror. Telling Joe had been her only real choice.

What Marissa hadn't been prepared for was the drop-dead gorgeous hunk she remembered from when they first met. It was the same night she wished a million times over that Molly hadn't been at the party. Her sister was three years older and always seemed to get what she wanted. And back then, it was Joe. It had been that way between them growing up, and then as adults.

Except when Joe left Molly. Her sister had been furious, but only because it made her look bad. There was no love lost between them, as Molly loved herself more than anyone else in the world. *Including Delia.* Which is why Marissa had become more of a mom to her niece than her own mother. Their parents had no control over Molly, and right up until the day they died in a plane crash, Molly benefited from being the spoiled child who could do no wrong. It was why as sisters, they'd never been close.

Marissa headed for the kitchen to wash the dishes. It only took a few minutes, and then she poured herself a glass of sweet tea, savoring the refreshing cold flavor. She made her way to the front porch and sat down on the swing, enjoying the gorgeous starry sky.

An hour later, she headed inside, refusing to stay up any longer and wait. As she started down the hall, the glimmer of headlights flashed through the living room window announcing his return. Resigned to the fact that the discussion would happen, she retraced her steps and sat down on the sofa. Luckily, Delia was fast asleep and wouldn't be any wiser about stage two of their discussion. *The nitty-gritty stage.*

"You're later than I expected," she said, when he came inside, his six-foot frame filling the doorway.

"I had an emergency that couldn't be helped. Why would Molly do this to me? She knew how much I wanted a family," Joe asked, cutting to the crux of the situation, as though it was the burning question he'd been asking himself since he left earlier.

It was the same question Marissa had asked herself over and over, but the answer never came. "I don't know. It was wrong of her and I'm trying to fix the wrong. I wanted the two of you to meet. Perhaps over the coming months, you can get to know each other. I'll take Delia back with me to Dallas and you can visit now and then. I'm the only family she's got right now, and stability is important." Laying the foundation of her expectations would make it so there were no assumptions to the contrary. She wasn't trying to dump Delia off. Quite the opposite.

Joe stroked his chin, deep in thought. "If what you're saying is true, *I'm* family."

"True. What I meant was that I'm the only family she knows and is comfortable being around. Also, I'd like to hold off telling her who you are until the time is right," Marissa added, knowing this would be a sore point, but one she needed his cooperation on.

Joe pulled back, the surprised expression on his face suddenly a dark scowl. "What do you mean? If you're so sure I'm Delia's father, then why the delay?"

He was testing her. "First, I know little about you, considering I haven't seen you in eight years. Second, this is an extremely sensitive subject to a young child and my biggest concern is Delia's well-being."

"It's a sensitive subject to a grown man, who might be a father, and who missed the first seven years of his daughter's life. I've thought about this, and I think you need to stay here for a few weeks and give me a chance to wrap my head around this. You're insisting she's my daughter, and if you're right, I've waited long enough to get to know her, don't you think? And I can't go running off to Dallas every weekend. I have a business to run, and I'm swamped. All. The. Time. You and Delia will just have to stay here until we can get this sorted out."

For a guy who didn't believe her claim, he sure was jumping in feet first. "Demanding much?" Hands on hips, she stared him down, unwilling to give an inch. *Yet.*

Joe stepped closer, the veins on his neck visibly pulsating with emotion. "Okay, two weeks. I deserve that much, don't you think?"

The problem was...Marissa agreed. Not that she would divulge that information. "It's not that easy. I work, and I'm behind schedule. My editor and the publishing house are already having fits, and I've promised them a rough draft in the next three weeks. I can't afford not to meet the newly revised deadline."

Joe rolled his eyes. "You're a writer?" The derision in his voice was crystal clear.

What a pompous jerk. "Yes. And what's wrong with that?"

Joe smiled, his warm brown eyes the color of milk chocolate. "Now that I think about it...nothing. It's perfect. You can write any-where, meaning my place is as good as back in Dallas. Not that I'm saying I believe any of this daddy business for a minute. It sounds like something Molly would concoct to get back at me for divorcing her."

Right now, no place was working when it came to writing. Never before had Marissa faced writer's block, but she was now. And Laura, her editor and best friend, was having a cow. It started when she found out her sister died in a car accident while jet-setting around Europe with her latest beau. And even though it had been only four months ago, Marissa had come to grips with the loss of her sister and to being a full-time mom. Despite all that, the words wouldn't come. "My sister made a lot of mistakes, and continued to make them, but she's still my sister. And I lost her, so please stop making remarks about her like that. We will never know why, but what's more important, is what happens next."

Joe nodded. "You're right. I'm sorry. This is just a lot to take in. Please, give me two weeks."

His plea was sincere, and it struck a chord in her heart. Not enough to change her mind, but enough to make her decision more difficult. "I can't. My publishing company reps aren't happy, seeing as I have nothing to show for the advance they gave me. And I can't give it back, now that I've got Delia to contend with and provide for." Sharing her financial woes hadn't been part of the plan, but he might as well know the truth.

Joe frowned; his jaw clenched tight. "It's just two weeks. And I'm not letting you leave with Delia. I can get a temporary injunction until a paternity test comes back if I need to, but I'm hoping you won't make me take that step."

He wouldn't dare. *Or maybe he would.* Was that even a thing? A temporary injunction that would force her to stay in Crossroads Creek? It didn't seem at all plausible, but it wasn't a chance she wanted to take. "I'll put a call through to my editor. If she agrees, Delia and I can stay in town and visit whenever you're available. It's the best I can offer. Take it or leave it." Truth was that she would stay, but she didn't want to make it too easy on the guy since he was playing hard ball.

"I told you I'm always busy, so it's just as well you stay here. Easier on everyone involved, and cheaper. And I'm sorry about tonight. It is the demanding part of my job and emergencies always seem to pop up when you least expect or want them."

Marissa shook her head. The temptation to stay here was strong knowing it would be a whole lot better on her bank account. "I can't do that. It wouldn't be right for us to live together, even under these circumstances."

"You're right, and I wasn't suggesting we live together. As I mentioned before, I'll stay in the bunkhouse. I'm gone a lot during the day doing rounds, but I would like to get to know the child when I find free time. As Delia's guardian, I'm guessing you are the primary caregiver either way, so nothing changes."

"Yes. Make sure you don't forget that." At least Joe understood that part of the equation. The other part was a slightly bigger problem. The truth was, after meeting Joe again, Marissa couldn't help but admire him. It was like having a crush all over again.

Only this time, her sister wasn't here to steal him away.

"We'll have to shop at the Super Saver tomorrow, as I don't have much food and most of what I do have is pretty basic stuff. So, what's Delia's name? Like her complete name?"

"Delia Rose Johnson. She was named after our grandmother. Feisty woman, and super independent, yet sweet as pie." Marissa smiled, fondly remembering her grandmother and the fact she had used her grandmother's middle name as her pen name. The woman's name she chose as a pen name when she started in the business.

"Pretty name. What's with her last name?"

"Molly took back her maiden name after the divorce."

"I see. Since you agreed to stay, I'll play by your rules. For the time being, anyway. It will give me more time to process what this would mean in my life," Joe said, giving in, but not graciously.

"I agreed to talk to my editor to see if I can get clearance," she said, reminding him she was still in control. It was a moot point, knowing she would stay, but she didn't want him to get used to calling the shots. They would need to learn to work together, and they might as well start at the beginning.

Chapter Four

♥

J OE WAS GONE AGAIN early this morning, with no set plan to return. Taking advantage of a few moments of peace and quiet, Marissa stared at her laptop hoping an idea would come to mind for the new story, but no words would come. She closed the lid just as Delia came in the room.

"Good morning, sleepyhead," Marissa said, as Delia curled up next to her on the sofa.

"Morning," she said, rubbing her eyes. "Where's Mr. Granger? He didn't come back last night. Doesn't he like us?" she asked, looking around the room.

Marissa smiled and hugged her niece closely. "Joe had a meeting last night and then an emergency call that kept him out late. He's an animal doctor and visits people on their ranches and farms. This morning, he had to work. And as to liking us...what's not to like?" Marissa grinned.

The handsome doctor was a busy guy, something she respected, but it wouldn't help them sort out what to do about Delia. Perhaps they could work out some sort of visitation schedule after she returned to Dallas. Once father and daughter were comfortable together, if Joe wanted every other weekend with Delia, Marissa wasn't opposed. As Delia's guardian and aunt, she would do her best to keep life emotionally stable for her niece.

"You're right, we are lovable. Except he didn't look happy that we were here. Why did you make me go play soccer when you talked to him? You only do that when you need to talk about me," Delia said, watching her closely.

The child was far too perceptive. "Joe was just surprised is all, which is a completely different thing. Mind you, he invited us to stay, so I'm thinking we are A-okay in his book. And I was just talking grown-up stuff." A bit of a stretch, but for Delia's peace of mind, it would work. A long time ago, Delia had asked about her father, but back then, Marissa hadn't known the truth, suspected. Not that she would have outed her sister and spilled the beans to a four-year-old asking the tough question.

"He must be a nice man if he talks to the animals," Delia said, her comment surprisingly spot on and deep.

"He's not Dr. Doolittle," Marissa said, ruffling the girl's hair.

"I like that movie. Maybe you could get it for my birthday?"

"Maybe. It won't be long now."

"How many more days is it?" Delia asked.

"Nine more days. It will go fast, trust me."

"Yay! And then I get to stay up later, right? Cause I'll be a big kid."

"We'll see. With school starting in a few weeks, you will need to be well rested to do your best each day. You love bringing home good grades, so it's a tradeoff," Marissa reminded her, knowing this was a discussion they had every couple of weeks, but the results didn't change. Not yet anyway.

"Which means no," Delia said, rolling her eyes. "That's not fair. When will Joe be back today?"

Marissa shook her head, more than a little used to her childish appeals and quick change in the subject. "I don't know. I'm sure he'll be back at some point. You wanted to explore so I'm guessing we have time to do that now."

"I thought you said we had to leave?"

"The plans changed last night. We're going to stay here for two weeks, if you don't mind, that is. Consider it your last hurrah before school starts."

"Really? That sounds like fun. Maybe Mr. Granger will take me with him to an appointment to see some animals. That would be so cool."

"I don't know. That's his job and there's no telling what it entails." The idea was for Delia to spend time with her father...not Marissa. Especially if she was to get any writing done. The problem was figuring out how to make it happen. "I'm thinking the answer would be no, but guess you could ask," she added, noting Delia's unhappy expression.

"Why wouldn't he let me? Other kids get to see grown-ups where they work. It's called...*hmmm*...let me think...it's like take your kid to work day or something like that."

Marissa choked on the seltzer water she was sipping. Talk about hitting the nail on the head. "Yes, I believe you're right." She doubted Joe would agree, but it would be a way for the two of them to spend time together...after Marissa had a few days to see for herself if Joe could be trusted to handle the responsibility that came with caring for a child.

Marissa waited until Delia had finished her breakfast and went outside to play before she called Laura. Dry Cheerios and more apples had been on the menu, but at least it was something. Now it was time to update her editor on the change in plans, and hopefully, as her best friend, she would understand the decision to stay in Crossroads Creek for a couple of weeks. Although what good would it do if the man was never around?

"Hey, girlfriend. What's up? Hopefully, you're home and have some chapters for me."

Straight to the point, as always. "*Umm*, no on both accounts. There's been a change in plans," Marissa said.

"What do you mean? You were supposed to get back and get started on the book. You promised."

"I know what I promised, but the meeting yesterday didn't go as planned. I couldn't have foreseen that Joe Granger didn't want me...I mean us, to leave. He insisted on getting to know his daughter. Well, his possible daughter." It sounded lame even to Marissa's ears.

"Possible? I thought you said—"

"I did say that Joe is her father, and I believe Molly and the birth certificate. Joe, however, doesn't put as much stock in Molly's claim. He wants proof of paternity. I feel sorry for the guy. I mean, seven years is a long time to miss out on your daughter growing up because of someone's vindictiveness. Especially knowing it was my sister who pulled this hateful stunt." Which was the only probable reason she agreed to this madness. *Guilt*.

"Interesting. So, is the guy cute? Married? Employed?" Laura asked, skipping to what she now perceived might be responsible for Marissa's change of heart.

Laura was way off base on this one. "He's my sister's ex-husband. Your questions are wrong on so many levels."

"Says who? They were divorced like eight years ago. And I still remember you telling me once how you met him first and your sister swooped in like she always did to one-up you."

Marissa sucked in a deep breath, not remembering she'd shared that sordid piece of the past, not even with Laura. "Which changes nothing. Poor guy had a bit of a shock tonight. Molly must have really done a number on him because it would seem he's still single and no kids."

"Interesting. I'm guessing handsome as well, since you said nothing to the contrary. For someone you've not seen in eight years, you seem to care a lot about his feelings. Did he remember you?"

"First off, I care because of what Molly did and because Delia has the right to know her father. I only met him once at the party, and then later, at their wedding. Molly and I didn't run in the same social circles. He vaguely remembered me, I think."

"The plot thickens."

"Stop. Second, I'm too busy to date. I've got an editor freaking out because I don't have a story even started yet and it was due two weeks ago."

"Well, there is that." Laura laughed. "So, have you thought of a storyline yet?"

She hated letting Laura down on a professional level. Writer's block had never been an issue, and Marissa knew Laura would take the heat for her delay. "No. I'm hoping while I'm here, I'll think of something. If I dictate the story, I can get you a rough draft sooner. Hopefully, that will appease the publisher and get them off your back until I can rewrite it."

"None of which happens until you have a plot. I know...what if you romanced Mr. Instafamily Daddy in your book? You would have some amazing material to work with right in front of you. You just need to create some fictitious woman he can fall in love with. I think it's perfect."

Marissa rolled her eyes, knowing her friend couldn't see her. "I think you're crazy. I'll think of something, Laura. I promise." The problem, however, was that deep down, she wasn't so sure it was true.

"That's what you've been saying for the past four months. I get that Molly's death has thrown you a life altering curveball, but it's time to get back on track."

"I'll think about it. Gotta run and check on Delia. Not to mention, try to figure out something in the way of an outline for the story," Marissa said, eager to get off the phone and end this discussion about Joe.

"I'm serious, Marissa. Romance the guy in a novel. It's perfect. And while you're at it, consider yourself for the position of heroine," Laura said, before disconnecting the call, cutting off any chance of a rebuttal.

Marissa was more than a little furious when Joe never bothered to show up today. The whole reason for them staying was for Joe to be able to get to know his daughter. Except if the absentee father didn't stick around long enough for that to happen, then Marissa's decision to stay was pointless. They could just as easily do the absentee thing if she returned to

Dallas. Though being fair, her writer's block might not step aside at either location.

They'd explored the areas closest to the house, and even visited the barn. It was odd to see it empty considering Joe's love for animals. She would have thought he'd at least have a horse. It was something she would have to ask him about later. Lunch wasn't very exciting, seeing as it was pretty much a repeat of what they ate before. Luckily, Delia could eat tomato soup until she turned orange, since it was one of her favorite meals. For dinner, she'd found some frozen ground beef, thawed it, and made bunless cheeseburgers for all of them, figuring Joe would be hungry when he did finally come home.

Delia had long since gone to bed, full of questions that Marissa didn't have answers to. While she waited for Joe, Marissa was more than prepared for the discussion they needed to have to set things straight.

She spotted two bright headlights shining through the front window as Joe pulled up in front of the house. It was about time he got home after missing the entire day. Marissa made her way out onto the front porch, trying to catch him before he headed to the bunkhouse. "Joe," she said, calling out to him as he rounded the truck.

He looked up, running a hand through his hair. "Good evening. It's been a long day, and I'm bushed." Joe checked his watch. "What are you still doing up?"

"Waiting for you. We need to talk," Marissa said, tired but needing to address this issue of the absentee father not fixing his schedule to be home more. It is why she agreed to stay.

"Can it wait? I'm exhausted and tomorrow's another day." Joe removed his cowboy hat and ran a hand through his hair with the crook of his arm.

"No. That's exactly what we need to discuss. Tomorrow, that is."

Joe let out a heavy sigh and moved closer to the steps. "Okay, then. What's up?"

"The fact you weren't around at all today. I didn't agree to stay here just to sit and do nothing. I can do that in Dallas."

"I'm sorry. Everything happened so suddenly and I'm doing the best I can. Rearranging my schedule takes time and I'm working on getting some things in place to help lighten the load. You wouldn't want me to slack off on my job and leave my clients hanging, would you?"

"Well, no. But get someone to help you. Most people have a backup. You can't run a business as a one-man show."

"Trust me, I know. My partner just retired, and things are hectic. The timing of your arrival is less than perfect and finding someone is exactly what I am trying to do."

Marissa shook her head, his comment rubbing her the wrong way. "I could leave. I didn't know there was any perfect time to introduce a daughter you didn't know about."

"I'm sorry. I didn't mean it that way. All I'm asking is for you to give me a little grace for a couple of days as I work things out."

Marissa didn't want to like it, but he was right. She was being unreasonable. "Fine. Just be around more tomorrow, for Delia's sake. She noticed your absence and questioned whether you even like us."

Joe nodded. "I see. The mind of an almost eight-year-old. Something I need to learn to understand. Point noted. And you were wrong about the no-good time to introduce a daughter, and it's not what I meant at all. In fact, anytime is better than not knowing."

"Well, okay, then. We'll see you in the morning." The guy was stressed over the sudden changes in his life, and to be fair, she recognized the magnitude of what he faced. Emotionally and professionally.

She hadn't gotten any writing done today while keeping up with Delia in their new surroundings. Hopefully, tomorrow would be better.

Chapter Five

J OE ENTERED THE HOUSE through the back door, the smell of strong coffee brewing in the kitchen, just the wake-up call he needed after another rough night in the bunkhouse. Hopefully, Marissa wasn't one of those '*faint at heart*' brewers when it came to coffee. He was more akin to the '*put hair on your chest*' strength when it came to how much ground chicory he used and didn't relish having to change.

Sip by sip, the fog in his brain lifted and last night's conversation with Marissa came to mind. She wasn't thrilled with his absence yesterday, but at least she understood he was working. It didn't change the outcome, and for

Delia's sake, he would do as Marissa asked and attempt to rearrange his schedule to spend more time with her.

Joe knew little to nothing about the child, other than the fact that she had her mother's face and hair, his eyes, and loved soccer. Not that he was certain about his apparent fatherhood, but some things pointed in his direction. The one time he'd seen Molly and the guy she was cheating with was an image he would likely never forget, and Delia looked nothing like the guy. The man's groomed jet-black hair, chiseled jaw, and refined features, including his tailor-made suit, spoke of wealth and society, something Joe never aspired for, much to his wife's consternation. *Ex-wife.*

Joe refilled his cup and turned to sit back at the table, surprised to find he wasn't alone. Delia's eyes were wide as she approached, her pink kitty cat pajamas making her look far younger than her age. "Good morning, Delia. You're up early," he said, searching for something to say.

"Aunt Marissa says I'm an early riser. I think it's because my eight o'clock bedtime is too early," she said, a knowing smile on her face.

As opposed to the childish PJs, Delia's comment was quite grown up, her reasoning spot on. "Perhaps. Have you discussed this with your aunt?"

Delia shrugged, hands on hips, and nodded. "Many times. But it's like she's stuck in toddler land when it comes to my schedule."

It was an expression he'd never heard, and it sounded like something she picked up at school. "Well, perhaps the two of us can talk to her about it." Not that he would interfere, but maybe to get the logic behind an early bedtime. Though to be fair, it's not like he knew the first thing about raising kids, and it looked like he needed a fast education on the subject.

"So, what's for breakfast?" she asked, plopping down in a chair next to him.

"I don't know. I don't normally eat breakfast. I could whip you up some box mix pancakes, I reckon." There wasn't much to choose from, something he meant to take care of yesterday but that never happened.

"My aunt says breakfast is the most important meal of the day. You shouldn't miss it. And I can't have gluten. Dr. said I have Celi something. I hate that word. It means I don't get to eat a lot of good things I used to eat."

"Celiac disease?" Joe pulled back, surprised by the news. It was a hereditary condition and one he had, but then so did lots of other people. It didn't mean they were related.

Delia nodded.

"I see. Lucky for you I have gluten-free mix." It was a coincidence and not something he wanted to let drop just yet. Marissa would be sure to connect the dots he wasn't willing to connect. He pulled open the refrigerator door, only to discover he was out of milk. "Sorry, I'm out of milk so no pancakes."

"You could fix me some eggs. Those are yummy in my tummy. Just no toast, unless it's like sourdough or gluten-free."

Last time he checked, sourdough bread was a no-no. "Why is sourdough different?"

Delia shrugged. "I don't know, I'm just a kid. But Aunt Marissa lets me have it once in a while."

"Eggs it is then." Joe was wishing Marissa would show up soon, as he was in over his head. "How do you like your eggs?" he asked, for the lack of anything better to say. Delia was like a young kid on older kid mode most of the time.

"Scrambled. Two eggs with yellow cheese, spinach, tomatoes, and okra if you have any. That's my favorite."

It was quite a list and very specific. His first meal with Delia was doomed for failure. "Sorry. I have nothing but eggs in the fridge."

"Fine. Regular eggs it is, but not runny. And do you have OJ?"

He nodded, relieved they had finally landed on something that would work. "That I can handle." Joe headed for the refrigerator and pulled out two eggs. He lit the stove and heated a small amount of olive oil.

Delia came to stand beside him. "And don't overcook them. They are like gross."

An almost eight-year-old telling him how to cook eggs...not exactly anything he expected to wake up to this morning. But then, nothing about his life was going as expected since Marissa showed up on his front porch with Delia. *His daughter.* Saying the word over and over still didn't make it real. "So, what grade are you in?"

"I just finished second grade. My teacher said I'm an excellent student, and she gave me a blue ribbon because of it," Delia added, smiling up at him.

"That's amazing. Nice job."

"Well, everybody got a blue ribbon, but I think she really meant mine."

Interesting point of view, though more than a little self-absorbed. Or perhaps a case of trying to feel special after her mother died. Dealing with the loss of a parent wouldn't be easy for a child. "Or perhaps everyone did so well that your teacher had a hard time choosing." He was in over his head for sure, but it sounded like the right answer. Where was Marissa?

"Good morning," Marissa said, standing in the doorway.

Prayer answered. "Morning. Delia wanted breakfast, so I'm frying her up a couple of eggs. Any interest in taking over? I've been instructed that they would be gross if I messed up." Joe grinned at Marissa, rather enjoying the view she presented. A white fluffy robe, her hair pulled up into a floppy sort of bun, zero makeup, and pink bunny slippers. Not at all what he expected from Molly's sister. The two of them couldn't be more different, something he had been noticing from the moment he met Marissa.

"I'd rather watch you in action," she said, pouring a cup of coffee and taking a seat.

"Suit yourself." He cracked the eggs, dropping them in the oil, taking extra care not to splatter the oil or break the yolks.

Joe handed Delia a fork and napkin and then got her a glass of juice.

"Aunt Marissa, Mr. Granger agrees my bedtime is too early."

"Oh, he does, does he?" Marissa frowned.

"That's why I got up earlier than you," Delia said.

"I see. What else did he say on the subject?"

"I'm standing right here. I said we should discuss it with you, that's all. Not trying to overstep my bounds," Joe added.

"Good to hear, considering I'm her guardian. Don't tell me how to parent my niece please."

Someone woke up on the wrong side of the bed...either that or her feathersruffled easily. Joe wasn't sure which. "Gotcha. I'm just helping her express her feelings on the subject." There was no reason for her to be on edge. She had only been Delia's guardian for a few months, so why would she care if he offered to help?

"It's hard enough to parent a child without conflicting opinions confusing Delia."

"Duly noted. I'm trying to do my best here and I'm flying blind."

"Try harder, and while you're at it—you might want to extinguish the fire on the stove and start over."

Joe whipped back to the stove just in time to see flames licking the oil. He slammed a lid on top of the pan and turned off the gas burner. His phone rang, and he pulled it from his shirt pocket. "What's up, Willie?"

"Something's wrong with Lady. She's laying down in her stall and her breathing is labored. She doesn't eat much, and she seems restless."

"Could be colic. I'm on my way." Joe hung up the phone. He moved the pan with fried hard eggs to the back burner. "Sorry, kiddo. The eggs would be gross based on your earlier assessment. Your aunt will need to take over. Duty calls." Saved by the fire...literally.

"Bummer. When will you be back? I was hoping we could play soccer, or hide and go seek later," Delia said.

Joe paused at the door to consider the question, but didn't have much time. "I don't know. I'm the only vet in town and I'm covering for the vet in Wylie while he's out of town. I've got to go and then there's my own appointments." Ralph had set him up with an interview later this afternoon, so he'd have to be back for that. Joe was hoping it went well, but until then, there wasn't much choice...he had to leave. *Daughter or no daughter.*

"Don't forget what we talked about last night, Joe," Marissa said, clearly not happy with him on multiple levels.

"I promised to try. This is me trying, and putting the animals and my clients first, which still has to happen. I am working on getting more free time. Trust me." It was the best he could do on such short notice.

"Fine," she snapped.

Clearly anything but fine. Getting this upset over a discussion about bedtime didn't bode well when it came to trying to figure out the future plans regarding Delia. Her feathers were more than a little ruffled, they were wind-blown. It suddenly occurred to Joe her anger was more than likely also because he was leaving again.

Marissa moved to the refrigerator and took out more eggs.

"Can I go with you?" Delia asked, getting down from the table.

"No, I'm sorry. Sick and injured animals can be dangerous. I'll be back." Joe strode out of the kitchen and out the front door, hating the disappointed expression on Delia's face. Maybe there was more he should have said, but given he wasn't at liberty to reveal his identity as her father and use that as his ace in the hole to connect to Delia, he was at a loss.

And then there was Marissa.

They were both unhappy with his choices, but unless the interview went well, there was little he could do about it.

Joe hurried back to the house, knowing he was running late for the interview. He'd already had to reschedule it for today, and it wouldn't be professional to put the young woman off a second time. Carrie Bradley sounded promising when he glanced at her transcript, and knowing Ralph recommended her went a long way to easing his mind. This had to work...for everyone's sake.

He pulled into the driveway, his gaze landing on the convertible mustang parked in front of the house. The woman wasn't well versed in country living, dusty roads, or odorific barnyards, which was an immediate and resounding strike against her. Joe slid out of the truck and went around to meet her, except the blonde hadn't noticed his arrival. Far too wrapped up in her headset and music to realize he was even standing there. Strike two. She was already getting on his nerves, and they hadn't said the first word to each other.

Joe tapped her on the shoulder, causing her to jump. She pulled the headset off and shot him a wide smile, her pearly whites gleaming in the sunlight.

"I didn't hear you arrive. Sorry," Carrie said, opening the door and sliding out gracefully, her long legs revealed in shorts and her slim body accentuated by the tight cotton dress shirt she wore.

"My fault. Sorry I'm running a little late." It was, in fact, his fault, but still...it was only five minutes. Not enough that an interviewee should let her guard down. "I'm Dr. Joe Granger," he added, reaching out to shake her hand, but more than a little surprised when she awkwardly hugged him.

"Sorry. I misread your...never mind. Sorry," she added, shooting him another one of her bright white smiles. "I love your place. Would I get to work here with you?"

"No. Large animal country vets go to our clients. It's much easier than loading the sick animals on a trailer and hauling them here." *Something she should already know.*

"Oh, right. That makes sense. So what do you want to know about me? I'd love the opportunity to learn from someone like you. The hands-on approach would be great." She batted her eyelashes, leaving the impression hands-on held a wealth of meaning.

Strike three. "We can go over to one of the local farms and you can deliver a calf. It'll give me a chance to see you in action. I'm sure Roger Haskins wouldn't mind a free house call to deliver his calf. He called not long ago and said it was almost time."

"*Ummm*, what exactly would I have to do? Like hold out my arms and catch the calf when it slides out?"

Book learning clearly didn't always translate to reality. Though he was more than a little curious why Ralph thought she was a good candidate. Unless...he was trying to do a little matchmaking. In that case, his friend was way off base on both scores. "Not exactly. Most of the time, everything goes well on its own. When there's trouble, they call me. As a vet, we might have to reach into the womb and turn the calf, or help pull it out, especially when there are twins. And we have to make sure the calves are breathing and check them out physically to make sure they are okay, and that the heifer is doing well. It's expensive to lose either, so we do everything we can to make sure that doesn't happen."

"So, when you say reach into the womb..." Carrie's expression was one of distaste and horror.

"Yes. You put on gloves and slide your hand into the backside of the heifer," Joe said, enjoying the delivery of the description far more than he should. Carrie needed to head back to school and perhaps consider becoming a small animal vet...or change careers. It would seem she missed some important classes in college. Veterinary work wasn't easy or pleasant all the time, and one had to have a strong stomach...or a deep-rooted desire to help animals. He fell into the latter category.

"I'm sorry, Dr. Granger, I don't really re-member that lesson and," she looked down at her clothes, "I'm not exactly dressed for that kind of interview. Maybe I could come back..."

It was no more than he already suspected himself. "That won't be necessary. I'm not sure you're a good fit for my practice here in Crossroads Creek, but I wish you the best. And as a piece of advice...dress for the position you want and always be professional." He hat-ed sounding like a father, but someone needed to clue the young woman in protocol.

"Sure thing. Thanks, Dr. Granger."

Carrie waved, jumped back in her car, revved the engine, backed up and was gone in a flash.

Joe shook his head. Twenty-one and green wasn't what he was looking for at all. They hadn't even started the interview, and she was three strikes and out. Once upon a time, he had been the college graduate and green, but at least he understood country life and his way around a cow. Something Carrie lacked. Nothing could make up for a lack of enthusiasm...or professionalism, and he didn't have time to babysit and teach whoever came to work for him. And most of all, Joe wanted someone who would fit into small-town living.

He'd let Ralph know it didn't work out and maybe try to find a graduate who had already done their internship and instead was ready to work on their residency requirement before they became a doctor.

Preferably, someone from a small town who already knew the ropes.

<h1 style="text-align:center">Chapter Six</h1>

WATCHING JOE FLIRT AND talk with the young girl irked Marissa to no end. It shouldn't matter, but it did. The girl couldn't be much over twenty. Not that she cared about what Joe did, but if his time was so valuable, then why did he have time to entertain?

Her sister had wanted the social party guy, and by the looks of things, Molly would have had her heart's desire with Dr. Joe Granger. The two of them had been better suited than either one realized while they were married.

Marissa shook her head, a sigh escaping her lips as she forced herself to focus on the blank screen in front of her. Thinking of him outside lollygagging did nothing for her attempts to write, especially knowing Delia was out back practicing soccer. Laura suggested she write Joe in as the hero character of her next story...but she wasn't seeing anything worth writing about. Admittedly, the storyline was a good idea, but that's where it ended.

She checked her watch and frowned. It was time to make lunch for Delia, even though Joe still hadn't made time for the shopping trip he promised. Tomato soup and apples were on the menu...again. At least they were something Delia loved, as apparently father and daughter had that much in common. There was no way to know what other similarities they might have, since they hadn't spent any real time together. Much more of this and she'd drive into town and buy the groceries herself and leave him to handle the explanations of her sudden appearance. *Much more of this*, and Marissa would take Delia and leave.

In the kitchen, Marissa heated the soup and fixed a couple of sandwiches. She checked on

Delia, surprised to see Joe talking to her. His daughter was explaining something about the ball and juggling, that much was clear. Minutes later, Joe headed for the barn.

Marissa stepped outside onto the back porch. "Delia, honey, lunch is ready."

"Yay. I'm starved," Delia said, rushing over.

"Good. Go wash up and I'll be back in a minute." She wanted a few words with Mr. *I'm Too Busy* and hurried after him. "Joe, wait up," she hollered.

He stopped and turned back. "What's up?"

"Certainly not you and finding time for your daughter. I thought we discussed this last night and agreed you would find some time to spend with her while we're here," she said, taking him to task.

"I'm working on it," he said, the defensive tone in his comment surprising.

Marissa wasn't about to be deterred. "Working on it, how? By flirting with some young girl? And right where your daughter can see you? How do you think that would make her feel if she saw you?"

"I wouldn't know, since you won't let me tell her that she is my daughter. *If* she's my daughter," he added, sticking to his original stance on the matter.

"I'm just trying to protect her. Is that so wrong?" Marissa asked.

Joe removed his cowboy hat and ran a hand through his hair, the veins on his neck popping with tension. "Except you're the one insisting she's mine. Clearly, you have some doubts as well."

He had a point...not that she agreed. "Well, no. I don't have doubts, but I do have doubts about your ability to parent. Maybe you're not ready to be a part-time instadad," she huffed.

"Really? It's not like I knew about her until a few days ago. And I'll have you know that the woman you saw isn't my arm candy or my date. Carrie Bradley is a Dallas University graduate, and she was applying to do an internship here so that I have more time for my daughter. Isn't that what you asked me to do?"

Marissa had stepped right into a cow patty mess. There was only one way out of her false assumption. "Yes, I did. And I'm sorry, I didn't realize."

Joe visibly relaxed. "Next time, ask before you malign my character."

"You're right, and again, I'm sorry. But do you always hug your potential employees?" Marissa asked before she could stop the words from escaping.

"Not at all. If you had watched more closely, you would have noticed she hugged me...not the other way around. And apology accepted," Joe said, forgiving her mistake.

"Oh, so, *ummm*, are you going to hire her?" Marissa was only asking because it would be great if he could spend more time with Delia, and nothing to do with the surge of jealousy she refused to own up to, should anyone ask.

"No." One simple word, but a wealth of meaning.

"And why is that?" she asked, her curiosity in overload.

"Because she wasn't right for the job. That's why most people don't get hired." Joe grinned.

"What more do you want in an assistant than someone well-versed in veterinary skills and just starting out to help you and hang on to your every word?" Marissa teased. So what if she was relieved that he wasn't hiring the beautiful blond?

"Someone that knows more than textbook skills. Someone not grossed out by the thought of helping animals when they aren't at their best. And definitely someone who understands the folks here in Crossroads Creek and treats them like friends, not just clients."

Marissa was speechless. This was a side of Joe she hadn't expected at all, and she couldn't fault him for wanting to keep his business more personable. "I see. What will you do?"

"I don't know. I've sent a message to Ralph at the university and I'm hoping one of the graduates who has already completed their internship might still be looking for a job as part of their residency requirement. Someone more well versed in small towns and large animals," he said, grinning at her.

Maybe there was a way for them to accomplish their objectives. Together. Not that she wanted to spend more time with Joe, but Delia's earlier suggestion made sense given the turn of events. It's not as if Marissa wasn't sympathetic to Joe's plight. "Why don't we make the rounds with you? Like the non-emergency calls. That way you are spending time with your daughter and your time with your clients doesn't suffer. I can even lend a hand if needed, if it's not too gross," she chuckled, quoting his words regarding the intern. "It might even be fun to learn more about what you do."

Joe shook his head. "No. Like I told Delia earlier, it can be dangerous around sick animals. They become unpredictable."

"But if we do everything you tell us to do, I'm sure we'll be safe. It's not like we are asking to walk into a Brahma bull pen while you do some sort of exam. Maybe the horses, cows, goats, or sheep. It would be an amazing experience for Delia." Not to mention the perfect research material for her book if she decided to write the story Laura suggested.

Joe nibbled on a piece of long straw grass he pulled from next to the fence. "Let me go on record that I think it's a bad idea, but I reckon we can see how it will go. What about your writing?"

"I'm at a standstill. I've had writer's block ever since Molly died. My editor seems to think I should write a cowboy story. If I learn more while I'm here, it would be fantastic for details and authenticity." She didn't normally discuss her writing with anyone, but then Joe wasn't just anyone. He was her niece's father and deserved more from her.

"Fine. Just so long as I'm not part of your research," he added, his gaze locked on her face for confirmation.

"Nope." She wouldn't need to research him, seeing as she was living in his house. Spending time with him would give her more than enough personality and traits for her character. The more she thought about it, the more Laura's idea took hold. And even if she did use Joe as sort of the idea, it would all still be fiction, considering she would need to create him the ideal woman that he could love and cherish forever. Joe would be the instigator, not the hero.

"If you're sure you and Delia are up to this. It's not a glamorous job by any means and can be quite boring if you're stuck watching," Joe said, still trying to dissuade her.

"I'm sure." And there was no denying the spark of excitement that settled in as she plotted out the story in her head. Words and ideas were rolling around at full speed. Perhaps Crossroads Creek was exactly what she needed to break the writer's block. Either that, or Joe Granger.

"Be ready to go in thirty minutes. Have you all had lunch?" Joe asked.

Marissa felt guilty. Not knowing what he was doing, she hadn't thought to ask. "Delia's eating now. There's enough soup for all of us and I there's a left-over burger from yesterday I cooked you for supper that you didn't get to eat."

Joe smiled. "Sounds good. After my last appointment we can stop at the Super Saver for some groceries. Thanks for putting up with the delay."

"Sounds good," she said, echoing his own words. At least he was willing to try it her way. Correction...Delia's way. She was only doing this for her niece.

Joe turned to leave but stopped. "One more thing. Can you get me Delia's hairbrush before we go?"

"What for?" It was an odd request.

"For the paternity test, of course. The sooner I get it sent in, the sooner we get results and can plan for the future."

Which meant what? It was no more than she'd been thinking, but hearing Joe say it was unsettling. She was the one in control of the situation.

"Sure thing. I can get you some of her hair from the brush since that's all you want," she said, stating the obvious. Marissa turned on her heels, and left, eager to tell Delia the good news. *And to make Joe's sandwich.*

Marissa didn't blame Joe for wanting the test. Given Molly's infidelity, it was prudent on his part, but one had only to look at Delia to know she was Molly and Joe's daughter. The little girl had so much of her parents in her personality and her looks.

What she wouldn't give to have her own family...complete with a loving husband. Her sister had been a fool to throw it all away, always instead searching for the limelight and something better.

Chapter Seven

♥

J OE RINSED OFF HIS plate and put it on the drying towel. "Thanks for the soup and burger. You spiced it up perfectly."

Marissa laughed. "Well, the tomato soup is all you have. I've never known someone to have like twenty cans of one kind and nothing else. It's all good though since tomato is Delia's favorite soup as well."

"I can eat the soup anytime, anywhere. That's cool Delia loves the same thing, but then two people can like the same things and not be related," he added, knowing what she was hinting at. And she didn't even know about the Celiac condition he shared with Delia.

"Perhaps, but the similarities keep building," Marissa countered, unwilling to concede this point or what she thought to be true.

Joe had to admire her tenacity. "So you keep saying. Time will tell. Are you both ready to go?"

"Delia said she had to grab something from her room. She'll be right along."

"Okay, then." He checked his watch. His appointment started in ten minutes, so he hoped *right along* meant one minute. He tamped down the urge to ask.

"While she's out of the room, here's the hair sample you asked for," Marissa said, handing him an envelope.

"Thanks. I'll take care of sending this off later today. I appreciate—"

Delia suddenly appeared, a flurry of energy as she bounded into the room. She had put on a long white sweater and...no way. A stethoscope?

"Great outfit," Joe said, grinning. There was no chance to finish his sentence with Delia back in the midst.

"If I'm going to be a doctor, I got to look like a doctor. Why don't you look like a doctor?" Delia asked, stopping in front of him.

"Vets, especially large animal vets, don't always wear a lab coat, unless there's a surgery of some kind and they want to protect their clothes. Most of the time, I wear a T-shirt and jeans. Comfortable and easy to clean."

Delia pulled off her sweater. "I've always wanted to be a doctor, but a doctor vet sounds way more fun. Can I listen to the animal's heartbeat?"

Joe laughed, pleased by her interest. "Nice career choice. And yes, I'm sure we'll figure out something so that you can listen to one of the calmer animals. Hearing a heartbeat like that for the first time can be inspiring."

"What's a career?" Delia asked.

The kid was full of questions...though good questions, this last one a reminder she was still quite young. "The job you decide to do when you get older."

"Oh. Then, yup. I'm gonna be an animal doctor for my career," Delia announced, sure of herself.

Marissa joined in the laughter and stepped forward. "The apple doesn't fall far from the tree, or so it would seem."

Joe nodded. "Perhaps. Kind of nice." His heart swelled with pride at the thought of his daughter having the same love for animals and medicine that he had. *Possible daughter, he mentally corrected.* "We've got to go."

They piled into his truck, Delia in the middle. Her hair smelled of fresh peaches and strawberries. Dressed in blue jeans and a pink top with a glitter butterfly on the front, her hair neatly pulled into a ponytail, she was the epitome of youthful cuteness.

"Our first appointment is at the Devoe Farm. They raise horses and have a training center. This is a routine vaccination for all horses over two years old."

"What's a vaccination?" Delia asked.

"Doctor shots." Joe shot her a wink, loving the way her eyes sparkled with inquisitiveness.

"That doesn't sound like fun. Why do they need shots?"

"The Devoe family breed their horses, which means they raise foals. Baby horses," he added for Delia's benefit and to ward off an extra question.

"That sounds lovely," Marissa said. "I always see the huge horse farms as I'm driving through the country. The white fencing set against rolling green fields that some places use can be so picturesque. And if you're lucky enough and the horses are up close...it's such a treat to watch them."

"You love horses?" he asked, somewhat surprised, seeing as Marissa came across as a city girl. Her tan slacks, dress flats, and white silk blouse were more suited for the office than doing rounds with a vet where one might get dirty. There was a high probability of her taking home more mud than when she arrived.

Marissa nodded. "I do. I've always wanted to learn how to ride, but it never seemed to be the right time."

Interesting. The light in her eyes matched Delia's, giving proof of her sincerity. "Maybe while you're here, we can arrange for you to finally get to ride a horse."

"Really? That would be amazing," Marissa said, awe in her voice.

"Is this for research? Or is it for you personally?" he asked, still not entirely convinced. It didn't matter, but he really wanted to know. He also knew what he wanted her answer to be.

"This is for me. Finally, my dream come true." She grinned, brushing back her hair off her face and glancing out the window, but not before Joe noted the blush in her cheeks.

"And me, too. Right? Can I ride, Mr. Granger?" Delia asked.

Joe nodded. "Sure thing. I'll ask Mr. Devoe and see what we can set up. Perhaps a stop at the five and dime will net us some more appropriate footwear for next time we visit here." Joe fell silent the rest of the way to the farm, his thoughts on Delia's comment. *Mr. Granger.* For so long...he wanted to hear the word daddy. If Delia was his daughter, would she ever call him that after he had been absent from her life for so long? Would she blame him for not being around? And how much did you tell an innocent young girl who wasn't part of her mother's evil manipulation?

These are things he hadn't considered. The one thing he had thought over...many times, and the answer didn't change. He wanted Delia to be his daughter more than anything in the world. He would make it work, for both their sakes. Molly, on the other hand, might take him a long time to forgive. That and a lot of prayers. Right now, it was still too fresh...and undecided.

He parked near the barn and slid out of the truck, grabbing his medical bag from the back seat. "This way, ladies."

Delia skipped up next to him and reached for his hand. It took Joe by surprise, but he rather liked the feeling of being connected to her. Would the feelings be this strong if she weren't his daughter? Or did it even matter? Bonding with a child who looked up to you was empowering and more than a little satisfying.

Wade Devoe came out of the barn and waved.

"Hey, Wade. I hope you don't mind, but I brought some assistants with me today. I promise they won't interfere, and I'll keep them out of the horse pens and away from Atilla. This is Delia, my vet in training," he put a hand on top of her head, "and this is Marissa. She's a writer getting research material for a book she's writing. They are visiting from Dallas for a couple of weeks." Joe had no intention of sharing too much about Delia at this point, not until he knew more answers.

Wade extended his hand, a warm smile of greeting at the ready as he shook hands with both the newcomers. "Friends of Joe are friends of mine."

"Thank you. I promise we won't get in the way," Marissa added.

"Who's Atilla?" Delia asked. "Is he a mean boy? Or a mean doggy?" she asked nervously.

Joe laughed. "Nope. He's a mean Brahma bull. Best keep clear of the pasture all together so as not to get him stirred up."

"Yes, sir," Delia said, her eyes wide as saucers as she looked all around in search of the monster animal. "Do you have to do vet stuff to the bull? That would be scary."

"Not today, but sometimes. There are things we do to make it less dangerous, so don't worry," he said, trying to reassure her. There were always pros and cons with any job, but if you understood the help and healing you brought to the animals, it far outweighed the negative. Seeing an animal in pain or in need of help always had the power to make him dig deeper and try harder, no matter how long it took. It didn't always work, but he believed his heart for the animals made him more intuitive. Which is why he wanted someone with heart for the job to work with him, not just someone with the right credentials.

"Good. I don't want you to get hurt. I like you, Mr. Granger," Delia said, smiling up at him.

Her words set his heart to racing. Step one: Like. Step two: Respect. Step three: Love. Joe could be a patient man when something was truly important. And a relationship with his daughter hit the highest marks in his world. In truth, the steps could apply to any relationship worth having. Joe liked Marissa, and he respected her, but love? Doubtful, given the past. Two out of three wasn't bad when it came to having friends. Something he and Marissa would need to be if Delia was his daughter.

"Wade, I'll be in the barn checking over the horses and giving them their annual vaccinations if you need me. Ladies, follow me, and remember no touching anything unless you ask first," Joe admonished.

"Yes, sir," Delia said.

"Yes, sir," Marissa said, grinning at him.

She was a smart aleck, but it was cute.

"Best mind your p's and q's. He's a hard one to please," Wade teased. "Stop by the house when you're done for some cool lemonade, and we can settle up the bill."

Joe nodded. "Will do. Got something to run by you anyway," he added, remembering the conversation with Marissa and Delia on the way over.

Wade moved off and Joe pulled open the barn doors. The smell of hay and manure greeted him like a regular friend. Stall after stall, the long barn could house up to thirty horses at any time. "Let's start here with the colt." Joe checked the client file and scrolled down to find Santana, the youngest horse, and one that would soon find a new home.

"He's so pretty. Can I pet him?" Delia asked, moving closer, not a lick of fear, even though the foal was a lot bigger than her.

"Yes. Let him smell your hand first," Joe said, holding the colt in place to keep him calm.

"That's it. Nice and easy. Don't be afraid. He senses you like him and is lowering his head for you to scratch. Go ahead and gently rub him in long strokes down his forehead and to the muzzle. Like this," he said, showing her how first.

Delia laughed. "I like him too. I want a pony. It would be so cool to have my very own horse to ride." She reached up and hugged the horse's head.

Joe was about to stop her but left her alone as long as Santana didn't seem rattled.

"Can I have a horse of my own, Aunt Marissa? Please," Delia asked, her voice taking on a childish whine.

It was almost as if she knew what the answer would be. Interesting. Joe made a mental note of the ask.

"Sorry, honey. There's not much use for a horse in Dallas. But whenever we visit Crossroads Creek, I'm sure it can be arranged for you to ride."

If Delia was his daughter, the visits would be to Dallas to see her aunt, not the other way around. And Delia would certainly have a horse if she wanted one. Surely Marissa didn't expect him to want anything less than full custody. "I'm sure we can work it out," Joe said, earning a look from Marissa that would have iced over a pond.

After doing a thorough check of the horse and explaining the terminology to his willing listeners, it was time to prep for the vaccination.

Then rinse and repeat with the fourteen other horses here.

"Any more questions?" he asked.

"I think you've been quite informative," Marissa said, still jotting notes in her book.

Joe nodded. "Okay, then. If you'll step out of the stall while I do the vaccination, it would probably be for the best. Horses don't like shots any more than we do, and I want him to be super calm."

"Okay, Mr. Granger," Delia said, moving toward the stall door with Marissa.

"Call me—"

Marissa snapped to attention, sending him a warning glare.

"Joe." He hadn't planned on outing his identity before he even knew the truth, and Marissa's lack of trust stung. Joe was a far cry better than the formality of Mr. Granger, and if she was his daughter, was far more acceptable. And perhaps more likely to evolve into daddy one day. More reason to add another stop to their visit in town. While the ladies were trying on boots and hats, Joe planned to mail the hair sample to the testing center at the post office. He had printed off the forms last night and filled them out, and the agency said it would take a week to ten days to get the test results back after he submitted DNA samples from both him and Delia.

"Wait," Delia cried out, moving back into the stall.

"What is it, sweetie?" Marissa asked, concerned.

"If Santana's going to get a shot, I need to listen to his heart first," she said, holding up her stethoscope.

Joe nodded, grinning like a proud parent. "You're right. Good job, Delia."

The young girl beamed under his praise. "Where's his heart?"

"Right here," Joe said, pointing to the left side of the horse's belly, just behind the left leg. "We can check the pulse in a few places, but this is the method I prefer."

"Can I listen?" she asked, holding up the end of her stethoscope.

"Absolutely." He moved her hand to the proper position.

"I hear it," she said, awe and wonder in her voice.

He loved Delia's vibrant personality, and the fact she didn't back down from learning new things. A trait he'd like to think she got from him.

Chapter Eight

♥

MARISSA WANDERED AWAY FROM Joe and Delia as they made the rounds. In a clear case of awestruck, her niece insisted on staying with Joe since she was the doctor's assistant. But then Delia didn't have a father figure in her life, and it was to be expected that her niece would thrive on the attention.

It was more than a little interesting watching Joe with Delia. They shared a sense of humor and almost a natural bonding, something else Marissa hadn't expected to happen, and definitely not this fast.

Marissa walked the length of the barn, checking out each horse and absorbing the sights and sounds. There was a peacefulness about the place that was hard to describe, but it was a feeling she hadn't felt in a long time. It was as though the rush of life slowed down, the neigh of a horse soothing. The few that stuck their inquisitive heads over the stall door, she stopped to stroke their forehead, talking to them randomly.

And while Delia was wowed by Joe, Marissa didn't have the same warm and fuzzy feelings. His earlier comment about Delia possibly getting a horse, almost as though she would spend more time in Crossroads Creek than Marissa originally expected, had rattled her.

More and more, she wondered what would happen when they found out the results? Would he try to take her away? And what were the rights of a father who never knew his daughter existed? It wasn't like he walked away, and Molly couldn't find him. Her sister's ultimate selfish act and lies were meant to deprive Joe of his daughter. And here she was...doing the ultimate selfless act to bring the two together, and now, she was left wondering if it meant she would lose custody. *Surely Joe would never go that far.*

The two of them needed to talk, but part of her feared what Joe might say. And what if Molly was wrong? The tiny seed took hold, and grew, as Marissa was faced with the emotional upheaval that came with the idea of losing Delia. Her tiny family circle was all she had after her sister died.

Seconds later, she felt guilty for even thinking that way. If Delia wasn't Joe's daughter, her beautiful niece would never know her father. Talk about being selfish. Deep down, she truly believed Joe was Delia's father and it would be such an amazing life-changing event for her niece. One that Marissa would never deny the child.

"Aunt Marissa, we're done," Delia called out, breaking into her wayward thoughts.

Marissa headed back to meet them, watching as Joe put away the medical supplies. "Wonderful. Did everything go okay?"

Joe nodded and shot her a smile. "Right as rain."

"I got to listen to lots of hearts. So cool. And now I'm thirsty. Mr. Devoe said we get lemonade. Yummy in my tummy." Delia laughed.

"Did you get more ideas for your research?" Joe asked, his over six-foot frame within inches of Marissa when he stood up. Close enough that she could smell his woodsy cologne. His jeans and white T-shirt fitted enough to show off a man used to hard work.

"I did. It will take some creativity to describe the sense of peace within the four walls of the barn. Or maybe the words will magically come to mind when I write." One could hope, though right now, it was thoughts of Joe that filled her head.

Joe pulled the barn door open, letting them pass through. He closed it behind them, and they headed for the main house, where Wade met them on the porch.

"Saw you coming. It's a beautiful afternoon, and I thought we could sit outside and enjoy the sunshine's warmth under the fan to combat the heat. Lemonade always seems to make it cooler. My wife Courtney, loves it out here."

Joe nodded. "Sounds good to all of us. Delia worked hard and needs refreshment."

Wade grinned. "Is that a fact?"

"Yup. And I got to listen to the horse's heartbeat. I love Santana. He's the best," she said, her eyes still lit up with excitement as she raced up the steps and plopped down on the porch swing.

"That's pretty cool," Wade said as he moved to the table to pour the lemonade.

Marissa sat in a lovely white wicker seat that had a blue and cream plaid cushion that looked inviting and comfortable. "I love this porch and furniture. I need to make a mental note for the future. Maybe if I ever buy a home, I can have this set up." She grinned.

"Courtney's the mastermind on that kind of stuff. I tried my hand at it once and was forced to promise to never try again." Wade laughed. He handed out the drinks, one by one.

"I'm going to be a vet just like Mr. Grang...Joe," Delia said, correcting herself.

Joe sat next to Delia on the swing, her niece beaming. It was as though he hung the moon. *And maybe he did to his daughter.*

"Wow. Starting her young, Joe. Good deal," Wade teased.

"Joe...don't forget to ask...you know what," she said, poking Joe's knee with her hand.

"Ask what, young lady. I reckon you could do the asking since it sounds like something you want," Wade said, winking at Delia to ease her fear.

Not that her niece had any fears, least ways, none Marissa knew of.

Delia glanced at Joe, and he nodded in approval. "Well, it's actually for me and my aunt. We're hoping we can visit again and ride horses before we go back to Dallas. Please," she added, hopping up from the swing to push her plea forward.

"We understand if you're too busy," Marissa added, not wanting to overstep their bounds or embarrass Joe.

Wade nodded. "Of course, you can come ride. We have a few horses that are only for training new riders. Just let me know before you head this way, and I'll double check to make sure there aren't other lessons planned."

"Yes! Did you hear that, Joe? I get to ride." Delia's face was flushed with excitement. "I can't wait."

"I heard it, and so did all the horses in the barn," he teased.

"Thank you so much." Marissa was just as excited but refused to do a happy dance like her niece. Though refined joy never did it justice.

"My pleasure, ma'am." Wade tipped his hat in her direction.

"Now that we have that decided, perhaps we could settle up today's bill with those lessons," Joe said, appreciating his friend's warm welcome and efforts to make the ladies happy.

Wade's gaze narrowed. "That's hardly in your favor and you know I like everything on the up and up."

"It's not about who's favor...it's about good will and helping one another. Neighborly," Joe added, trying to convince his friend not to push back on generosity freely given.

"Sounds old school, but then, I am old school." Wade chuckled. "I won't say no. Expenses for the horses keep going up every year."

Joe nodded. "Don't I know it? I'll call you tomorrow and see what we can work out. Right now, I've got to take them into town to do some shopping. It would seem they aren't impressed with my bachelor's selection of food. And I'm not impressed with their riding footwear and outfits," he said, shooting a wink in Marissa's direction.

"Sounds about right," Wade said.

"Thanks for the lemonade. It was deeelicious," Delia said, rubbing her tummy. She jumped down from the swing and ran off the porch.

"Thanks for everything," Marissa said, following Joe's lead as he stood and made his way down the porch steps. "Hope I get to meet your wife when we come back." She shook hands with Wade, Joe doing the same.

"Talk to you tomorrow. And thanks," Joe said.

He drove into town, stopping in front of the five and dime. "Why don't you shop for the clothes first so that the food will stay cold until we get it home?"

"Great idea," Marissa said.

"Aren't you coming in?" Delia asked, when he didn't follow them inside.

"No, just tell Betina what you need, and she'll point you in the right direction. Tell her to put it on my bill. I've got to run to the post office and the bank."

Marissa shook her head. "I can pay for our—"

"I'm sure you can, but all things considered...I would like to buy you the proper boots and attire. And get a hat to complete the ensemble. I'll be back in about twenty minutes if you need help, and to make sure you follow my instructions," he teased.

And with a tip of his hat in Marissa's direction, he was gone, envelope in hand. Marissa knew where he was headed, and what he was mailing, but it was best not to dwell on it.

"Come on, let's go find us some new horseback riding attire." It would be fun to shop and not worry about the expense and how much of her advance she was eating into.

The wait at the post office to certify the envelope took a lot longer than expected. He stopped by the bank to make a deposit and then headed for the five and dime. The bell jingled overhead as he entered the store.

"Good afternoon, Betina. How's things going?" he asked when the older woman waved at him from the register.

"Good. Good. Your lady friend and her daughter are in the clothing section." She pointed to the back of the store, though it wasn't necessary.

"Thanks. I guess I'll check in on them and stick around till they finish up."

Joe made his way to the back, rounding the last aisle to find them laughing as they posed in front of the mirror. "Hello, ladies. Looking good," he teased.

Marissa spun around. "I didn't expect you," she offered, her cheeks bright pink.

"Look, Joe. Isn't my dress pretty?"

"It sure is. Purple is definitely your color." Whether or not it was, he didn't know, but a compliment was always in order.

"It's my favorite color."

Duly noted for future reference. "Did you find something to wear to go riding?"

"Yup. And I picked out the coolest boots and cowgirl hat. Don't you like Aunt Marissa's outfit?"

The loose-fitting skirt was a kaleidoscope of color, and the white gauze blouse with tassels at the neckline seemed quite carefree. "Actually, I do. It suits her personality." Joe grinned.

Marissa's hand went to her throat as though she were trying to hide, backing her way closer to the dressing room. "I'm guessing that's a good thing."

Why was she so unsure of herself and unable to take a compliment? It was something he'd have to ask her about. "Of course. Your creative nature is reflected in the colorful outfit. Not to mention the blue matches your eyes."

"Well, okay then. I'll change and we can leave." She disappeared behind the curtain.

"Can I get this dress, since you like it too?" Delia asked, looking up at him, a hopeful expression on her face.

"Of course. A beautiful girl always deserves a beautiful dress." He would buy her anything she wanted if it turned out she was his daughter. Only the best. And honestly, even if she wasn't his daughter, making her happy...made him happy.

"Delia, you need to change back into your clothes," Marissa called out.

"Yes, ma'am." Delia immediately went behind the other curtain to change.

Marissa was doing an excellent job of parenting, judging by Delia's immediate compliance without argument.

Something else he needed to remember.

Chapter Nine

♥

DELIA WAS A BUNDLE of energy and up earlier than normal this morning, knowing she would have her first riding lesson today. The problem was, she wasn't great in the waiting department. Hopefully, nothing would come up and Joe wouldn't get an emergency call. If he did, Marissa would be tempted to go without him. After all, he knew how to ride.

And there was no way she would miss this opportunity for a lesson. It was a dream come true for both Delia and Marissa.

Joe had said two o'clock, and they waited on the porch for him to arrive. A sense of déjà vu washed over Marissa. At least this time, there would be no life-changing surprises. Delia got up a dozen times to peer down the driveway, looking for signs of his arrival.

"Do you think he's not coming because of another emergency?" she asked, her voice taking on a slight whine.

Understandable, given she'd been anxiously waiting and dressed for the ride in her new outfit for the past two hours. "I'm sure he'll be here soon, honey." Faith in Joe's schedule was scarce, considering the line of work he was in. Always on call, and his job was so important to the ranchers, farmers, and their livestock.

"There he is," Delia shouted, pointing to the cloud of dust coming up the driveway.

Marissa let out a sigh of relief. Joe parked the truck and then headed their way.

"Who's ready to go horseback riding?" he asked, grinning at them.

"Me. Me," Delia said, raising her hand and jumping up and down.

"Don't you look the part. Love the jeans and boots, and that hat—so totally you. Sits just right," Joe said, pulling Delia in for a hug.

"Thanks," Delia beamed.

"You look like a natural cowgirl, Marissa. I'll take you riding anytime you want to go." Joe grinned, offering her a hand as she came down the porch, admiring her ensemble.

Marissa blushed. "Thanks."

They headed for the truck. "You don't take compliments well. Why is that?" he asked, more than curious for some time now.

Marissa shrugged. "I don't know."

"You can do better than that. Spill," he said, as they climbed in the front seat, and he came around the other side.

"Let's just say I was a late bloomer, and kids teased me. And then to top it off, my teachers and professors in my early writing stages didn't appreciate my style and stories. They continually gave me poor grades."

"I see. Well, I'm glad you didn't let them stop you. I'll just need to compliment you more often to make up for their poor guidance."

Marissa laughed. "I'm okay. Don't be nice on their account."

"I'm not. It's on my account as I find you to be a likeable person," Joe said, shooting her a wink.

It wasn't long before they arrived at the Devoe riding stables, and Wade met them out front.

"Good afternoon. Glad we could work this out for today," Wade said, shaking hands with Joe.

"Where's my horse?" Delia said, unable to contain her excitement as she looked around. "Is he a big and tall horse? That might be a little scary."

Wade laughed. "No. For your lessons, I've got Angel and Oatmeal. Two great beginner horses that know the ropes and are patient."

"That sounds good to me," Marissa said.

"Joe, I thought you might give me a hand. I'll work with Delia if you want to work with Marissa."

"Sounds like a plan," Joe said, moving closer.

"Great. You can just mirror what I'm doing so that we can keep them at the same progress level."

"So, are we going on a real ride? Like out there?" Delia asked, pointing out to the pasture.

"No. We start with the basics in a few lessons. You need to understand how to ride, and how to respect the horse, before you tackle going on a ride. Any other way would put the cart before the horse," Wade said, laughing at his joke.

"But how can you put a cart before a horse? A cart can't pull the horse," Delia said, completely confused.

Marissa and Joe laughed.

"It's just an expression, honey. It means you need to learn to ride before you can ride," Marissa explained.

Delia shook her head. "Grownups can be so confusing."

"This way, Delia." Wade led them around to the side of the barn.

A small, white mare was tied to a post, a slightly larger brown mare next to her.

"Meet Angel and Oatmeal."

"Oh, they are so pretty. Can I pet them? Joe showed me how already," she said, showing off her newfound knowledge. "And I know Angel's heart is right here," she said, pointing to the area where Joe told her it was located. "I remember from yesterday."

"Good memory. Go right ahead, pet her forehead and muzzle. Angel loves attention." Wade pulled some small carrots from his pocket and started to break them up to feed the mares.

"Oh, can I do that? Feed them a treat?" Delia asked.

Wade handed Delia and Marissa a carrot. "You both get to. It helps let the horse know you're friends and helps you to bond before we put you in the saddle. Trust is a two-way street."

Marissa held out her hand, following Wade's lead. "Her nose tickles." She laughed.

"It does," Delia agreed, grinning from ear to ear, her eyes lit with excitement. "What's next?"

"Impatient little thing, aren't you?" Wade chuckled.

"She's been looking forward to this since you said she could ride," Marissa clued him in.

"Gotcha. Well, in that case, let's get through the protocol when getting on and off a horse and some of the basic riding skills. Then we can get you in the saddle for some practice and to work on walking a horse around the pen."

"So I do get to ride. Cool," Delia said, dropping a kiss on Angel's muzzle when the mare lowered her head.

Marissa and Delia listened as Wade and Joe explained the do's and don'ts of riding, and of course, went over a basic vocabulary list of horse terminology that she was sure would have to be repeated many times for Delia. There was a lot more to saddling and bridling a horse than she would have imagined. Her niece's rapt attention, however, was testament to how much she'd been looking forward to this moment.

"Any questions?" Wade asked.

"Can we go now?" Delia asked.

Marissa shook her head and frowned at the impatient request.

"Please," Delia added, smiling as though there were no regrets to her question.

"I reckon we're ready. Joe if you can help Marissa, showing her the proper technique from the left side, that would be great."

"Sure thing." Joe stepped forward to help Marissa as Wade took Delia's hand, and they moved a little farther away with Angel. "Are you okay with everything so far?"

"More than okay. Ready to ride, just trying to have more patience than Delia." Marissa chuckled.

"She's fine. Wade is used to it from other kids that take lessons. Most horses are trained for left side mounting, so stand here, put your left foot in the stirrup, and then push up to get your leg over the saddle, using the saddle horn to help pull you up. It's easier if you sort of push off with your left foot."

Marissa followed his instructions, and suddenly found herself sitting astride Oatmeal. It was a lot higher up than she expected. The mare shifted positions and Marissa hung on for dear life. "What do I do now? She's like moving around. What if I start to fall?"

"You'll be fine. Oatmeal knows what to do and she's quite calm. Look at Delia, she's up and Wade is already walking her around the paddock."

"Kids are fearless. Besides, she's closer to the ground," Marissa retorted, feeling slightly embarrassed.

"It'll be fine. Just stay upright and relax with each move. No reason to stay stiff and unyielding, but don't slouch either. That's it. Hold that position and press into Oatmeal's sides with your legs and say giddy up. She'll know to move forward."

The first few steps were nerve-wracking.

"That's it, you're doing great. Now put a little pressure on the left side of the rein against her head, that will get her to turn to the right. Exactly. Now try the other side."

"Nice work. To stop, you pull back on both reins slightly and say whoa."

Marissa couldn't believe how well the mare responded to the slightest touch of the reins. "Am I doing this right?"

"You're doing great. I'm going to lead you around the paddock a few times, and if you're comfortable after that, I'm sure Wade will be okay with you trying it on your own."

"Oh, I don't know about that. I don't want to rush things."

"It's all about trust."

"Trusting you? I do."

"No. Trusting the horse, but it's good to know you trust me," Joe said, grinning up at her.

The next hour went by quickly, but it was exhilarating. Marissa had no idea how much she would love riding, though she always suspected.

Delia, too, was hooked. When it came time to leave, she wasn't happy. But then, she was just a kid and enjoying something new, so it was to be expected.

Chapter Ten

♥

T HE PAST FEW DAYS settled into a routine that all seemed very surreal for Joe. It wasn't always easy, but he made sure to be home for dinner, and to have time to play with Delia. It meant rearranging clients and putting off the non-emergency visits, but so far, everyone was more than accommodating in trying to help cut back on his hours.

Some appointments, Delia and Marissa joined him. Others, it was just Delia so that Marissa could write. Delia listened well and was eager to please. That in itself made it easy to take her with him.

Truth be told...he rather enjoyed having them both around. It made his appointments more fun, and time passed quickly. It turned out to be a great way to spend more time with his daughter.

At least, that's what he attributed to his eagerness.

Admittedly, Marissa was equally fun to be around. Somewhere along the line, he stopped comparing her to Molly and stopped holding her responsible for Molly's actions. The two women couldn't be more different.

A couple of hours after Joe returned home from an emergency call, Marissa tucked Delia into bed, the little girl sleepy after a long day. At least they had time together and even ate dinner like a family.

It had been a long time since he could just sit back and relax, and he was hoping tonight would be uneventful. He looked up as Marissa joined him in the living room.

"We need to talk," she said, sitting at the edge of the sofa close to his chair.

Joe drew up one eyebrow, more than a little concerned by her soft voice that carried a hint of urgency. "What about? I thought the past few days have gone well and that you would be pleased."

Marissa shrugged. "They have been good, but there's something we should discuss without Delia around." She twisted her fingers round, massaging her palms, a sign she was highly agitated.

"Let's hear it," Joe said, his earlier excitement over the day dwindling.

"As you know, I brought Delia here to meet you. I think we need to discuss what happens when the test results come back. You know, like a visitation schedule after these two weeks are up."

"Well, it might take a few months to get everything straightened out, but perhaps we could do every other weekend. I will do everything I can to make this work. I promise."

"That sounds doable. I'm relieved to hear what you're thinking. I practically raised Delia as my daughter. Molly was always running off somewhere and dropping Delia off with me. Not that I minded, because I work from home."

His heart ached for Marissa. It would be a difficult change, and he would do anything to help her adjust, making sure she saw Delia often. "Do you regret bringing her here?"

Marissa shook her head. "No. You might not have ever known, but God would."

"Thank you. Your faith is a beautiful thing because it shows me who you are as a person. Doing the right thing isn't always easy, but a father should be there for his daughter, and I appreciate you giving me the chance to make this right by her." Marissa was an important part of Delia's life, and it was paramount they worked together in Delia's best interest.

Marissa nodded, letting out a deep sigh as she sat back on the sofa.

"Have you been able to get any writing done?" he asked, hoping for a change in subject. This couldn't be easy on her, but he was glad she trusted him and understood.

"Not so far. I told you about the writer's block, but there's more. Losing Molly and suddenly being a full-time parent for Delia…not to mention the expenses, has me worried about so many things. I've used up most of my advance on the book, so I can't give it back. I'm way past due turning in a fresh manuscript to my editor and the publisher says no more extensions. My career is on the line. Laura, my friend and editor, is the one who thought I should do a cowboy story, but I don't know. There's so much to learn." She let out a heavy sigh, the weight of the world on her shoulders.

"I'm sure you're an amazing aunt and an awesome writer. And I'll reimburse you for any expenses. As for the writer's block, I'm not sure I can help you there, seeing as I have no experience." Joe smiled, trying to lighten the mood in the room. "What kind of romance do you write?"

Marissa shook her head. "The happily ever after kind. And I write it, but like you, haven't found it either. It's not a prerequisite for writing books. The stories are about what it could be like if you found the perfect person...and life's challenges didn't trip you up. Hence the word...story." A gentle smile tugged at the corners of her lips. Talking about her work seemed to bring her joy.

"Too bad you didn't write murder mysteries or something along those lines. Then I might have been able to help with ideas. But in the romance department, love hasn't been my strong suit. Once upon a time I wanted love, marriage, and a family, but your sis—. Never mind," he said, realizing what he was about to say and preferring not to bring Molly into the conversation.

"If you really wanted a family, why didn't you get married again?" Marissa asked, skipping his close mistake.

Joe shrugged. "Once bitten, twice shy. That cliché says it all." He simply couldn't trust anyone with his heart again. But then there was Delia. She was creeping into his heart, threatening to bust open the wall he'd built around it. And then there was Marissa. Kind, sweet, and loving Marissa. Not right for him...but proof some women could make excellent decisions and therefore be reliable as a partner. Whoever swept her off her feet would be a lucky man. Unfortunately, it couldn't be him, not with Molly looming large between them.

"Too bad. You're good with kids. Delia is lucky to have you."

If she was his daughter. After today, he wondered if it even mattered. Delia had crept into his heart and even if they were wrong about him being her father, he would make time to see her again. The kid deserved love after what her mother put her through. And whether or not she was his daughter, she was conceived while he was still married to Molly. "Thanks. What about you?" Asking was dangerous territory, but he had to know.

"I've had a few terrible relationships, and I want more from love and marriage than it seems guys want to give. For now, I'm happily writing all the romance I can handle." Marissa laughed.

"I see. So, what pen name do you write under?" he asked, more than a little curious.

"*Umm*, I sort of ghost write for an author and I'm not at liberty to say," she said, surprising him.

He'd heard of ghost writing, but never really thought it was considered a full-time job. And why would a ghost writer get an advance? Or deal with editors and publishers. Clearly, it was a world he knew nothing about. "And you're satisfied with that? Never getting credit for your writing?"

"Yes and no. It's hard to explain. But I really don't like to talk about it since it's strictly confidential," Marissa said, gazing out the window at the moonlit sky.

In other words, subject closed. "I see. Well, I will pray your writer's block vanishes and your cowboy story comes to life. I've got a long day tomorrow. Good night," he said, rising to his feet.

"Goodnight, Joe. And thanks." Marissa stood, the top of her head barely reaching his shoulders in her stocking feet.

"For what?" Their nearness confused him. Why did he have the sudden urge to kiss her?

"A good day. Delia and you. I'm sorry if I sounded selfish earlier. It's just taking some time to get used to sharing her."

"It's all good. And...both of us will always be in her life. I promise."

"Thank you."

Mighty big promises for a guy who didn't have confirmation Delia was his daughter. With each passing hour, he wanted it to be true more and more. *A daughter.*

And then there was Marissa.

Chapter Eleven

♥

MARISSA STARED AT HER laptop, typed out a few words, and then hit delete. She tried again, typing a few words, staring at the page, and then hit delete. The cowboy story wasn't taking hold. She needed an emotional edge. Not just a good-looking cowboy who rides off into the sunset with a pretty girl from town.

Laura's words came back to her. *Write about Joe.* That's an emotional twist that will make the reader root for the hero and a happily ever after. It made sense. As for the fictional heroine, perhaps the girl-next door would work. Or maybe the server at the Main Street diner. She would change just enough of the story so that no one would know it was Joe...except her. And of course, Laura, but her friend would never reveal the motivational character.

If Marissa wrote the story based on reality, it would give her a script to follow. Which meant the story would practically write itself. And then her editor and her publisher would be happy, and Marissa's career wouldn't tank. The trick was to change just enough that it was still fiction but revealed the core of the hero.

"*Hmmm.*" She tapped her chin twice, racking her brain for a name. It was always a good place to start.

Joe Granger meet...David Forester. Good solid name for the lucky guy about to fall in love...Rose Bloom style. Even if only on paper. She typed the character's name and then filled in some details. Six feet tall, reddish-brown wavy hair, a broad chest. Cowboy who liked his jeans, T-shirts and hat. And always wore boots. Handsome was a given. Good with kids.

Hurt in the past. Easy to love if you looked past the exterior shield.

Now to figure out the right heroine for him. It would have to be someone very special, someone who equally deserved love. Which honestly, would include someone like herself, if not for the history between them. Neither of them were dating for much the same reason...both had no time, and both had been cheated on.

Not that she'd share the details of her sob story with Joe. It was just one reason Marissa didn't want anyone to know her pen name. The publicity would make her private life open to inspection. And now, more than ever, she needed to keep her private life private. Delia deserved that from her...an ordinary life after her not-so-ordinary childhood.

Jane Doolittle. Ha! Perfect for the vet. Marissa chuckled at the irony of the name she settled on. Perhaps a schoolteacher in Dallas. Or a photographer. Someone who loved kids, especially her niece. Not as tall, perhaps only coming up to David's shoulders. Blonde hair, blue eyes, and a heart of gold.

Next up, the story line. Where to begin. At the beginning, of course. The moment Jane arrived in Cades Cove. Marissa thought for a moment, her fingers poised over the keyboard. And then it clicked. Her brain swirled with ideas and thoughts she needed to capture. She outlined the book, point by point, chapter by chapter. It was only when she got to the last few chapters she stalled out. There was no way to know how the actual story would end, so she would have to make it up. Which wouldn't be a problem with everything else she had, and it was supposed to be fiction.

Excitement sizzled through every nerve of her body. It was always this way when she started a book...and all the way to the end. Complete with gut-wrenching emotions and tears along the way. She always figured...if she didn't cry writing the story, then readers wouldn't cry reading it. It was something she always remembered and strove to connect with her readers.

She typed without stopping, barely noticing the time. Three hours slipped away, and she heard Delia and Joe had returned, the sound of them talking and laughing breaking her out of her writing mode.

The two of them had gone to Joe's appointments together, letting Marissa stay home and write. She knew Delia would be safe with Joe and mind him well without having her tag along as backup supervision. Or possibly, she was operating on a bit of a disconnect mode to help ease her troubled heart once the paternity test results came in.

More than likely, it was a little of both. But now, finally, the ideas and desire to write were aligned with the time to write. It was a win-win situation.

She reached for her phone to text Laura.

Marissa: Doing the story your way...and it laid out beautifully. Outlined most of it today and will start the rough draft to-

morrow. *Hope to have it for you soon. I promise!*

Laura: *Awesome. And then you can come back to Dallas, and we'll celebrate. Rose Bloom is back! Yay! Perhaps another NYT bestseller is on the way...*

Marissa: *You never know. I just need the perfect heroine. ;) So far...her name is Jane Doolittle. Haha!*

Laura: *Too funny. I can think of a real-life heroine...just saying.*

Marissa: *No!*

It would be fun to pretend she was the heroine, but that risked Marissa becoming too involved and leaving her emotions hanging out to dry for all the world to see. *No way.*

By morning, she would have the perfect heroine for Joe. *David.* She just needed to sleep on it tonight and pray, and hopefully the heroine would develop right in front of her closed eyes. *Thank you, Theta waves.*

Marissa turned off the desk light and headed for the kitchen. A cool and refreshing iced tea sounded amazing as a reward for her productive finish to the writing session. She couldn't wait to tell Joe about the breakthrough. She poured a glass of tea and added ice, savoring the peach flavor. Joe had been resistant to trying a flavored tea but discovered something new he liked.

She glanced out the kitchen window and was surprised to see Joe and Delia playing soccer. They'd come in and gone back out without so much as a word to her. And they were having fun. Though being fair, Marissa hadn't even tried to play soccer with Delia, having never been into sports a day in her life.

Watching them laugh and run around tugged somewhere near her heart. Joe would be a great dad. And Delia was a great kid. So where did that leave her? She loved Delia as though she were her own daughter and couldn't help the jealousy of someone stepping in to fill her shoes. At least, when they left Crossroads Creek, Delia would leave with her. Over the past four months, they'd established a routine. And truth be told, the routines had been on again, off again for the past eight years. And then there was school starting back in a couple of weeks. There was so much he still didn't know or understand, and it was up to her to make sure she filled him in so that he made the right decisions.

Bottom line, they would need to work together for the best interests of Delia.

The back door opened and the two of them bounded inside.

"Hi, Aunt Marissa," Delia said, taking off her sneakers at the door. Something Joe taught her. But then, it's not like they had dusty driveways and horse manure clinging to their shoes back home.

"Hi, sweetie. Did you have a good day?" Marissa asked.

"The best. Right, Joe?" Delia beamed up at her new best friend.

"We sure did." Joe grinned.

"Joe said I didn't have to work as much as he did, so I took lots of breaks and played with people's pets. Everyone has cats and dogs and bunnies. I wish I had a pet. Oh, and I got to meet Mr. Wade's son, Trevor. He was visiting his grandparents when we had our riding lessons. He was at one of the places we stopped today visiting his uncle. Cool kid. He's like nine years old. At least I think that's what he said. We played soccer. That was super cool." Delia was bursting with energy, joy unleashed with every word.

Marissa smiled. "What an eventful day. Sounds pretty special."

"How was your day?" Joe asked, pouring two glasses of tea.

Marissa smiled, her excitement bubbling over much like Delia's. "I couldn't wait to tell you both. The writer's block is gone. I'm so excited. And I have the story mostly outlined, so tomorrow morning I'll hit the ground typing. My editor is so happy. I might even meet the latest extension deadline they gave me as an ultimatum."

Joe hugged her, catching Marissa off guard. "That's wonderful news! We should celebrate and go out for pizza tonight," he said, quickly stepping back.

"What a lovely idea," Marissa said, suddenly more focused on Joe's hug than her good news. Did he mean anything by it? Or just a friendly, happy hug? Probably the latter based on what he had told her. Which was for the best.

"I'm all in, in case you two want to ask me," Delia said, looking back and forth between her and Joe.

"I know you love pizza, silly," Marissa said, tousling her hair. "Will they have gluten-free crusts for Delia?"

"Absolutely. They have an excellent cauliflower crust," Joe said, wondering how soon Marissa would realize the truth about him and Delia having the same medical condition.

"Aunt Marissa, can I go to Mr. Wade's house and play with Trevor tomorrow? Joe called his mom, and she said it would be okay if it's okay with you," Delia asked, her soft smile a welcome sight.

Ever since her mom passed away, Delia hadn't tapped into spontaneous joy and suddenly, her easy-going good-natured character was back in place. It all started not long after they arrived in Crossroads creek, something else for Marissa to consider. "That's fine, honey. And Joe, I'm hoping I can join you on a few more appointments. I've decided the hero in my book will be a vet and I could use the research for some spot-on details."

"I thought you said the book wouldn't be based on me?"

"It's not you. The hero's name is David Forester. It's just easier to write what I'm experiencing."

"Well, in that case, you've got yourself a deal." Joe shot a wink in her direction that made her feel alive. It would seem Joe was influencing her and Delia.

She just hoped it wasn't a negative effect in the end.

Chapter Twelve

♥

PIZZA NIGHT HAD GONE off without a hitch. In fact, Joe couldn't remember the last time he laughed so much. And it was the oddest thing, but Delia's favorite pizza was the same as his...pepperoni, peppers, onions, and tomatoes. It wasn't a common combo, but her taste buds ran like his, apparently. And of course, once the server let slip about ordering the usual and that it was automatically gluten-free pizza crust, she grinned like a Cheshire cat licking up a bowl of cream.

This morning, however, was another matter entirely. Joe hadn't been able to bring Marissa or Delia with him because of the emergency call he received. A breeched calf could take hours and was messy, especially with twins. It wasn't something he could stop and explain, or something either of them would want to watch.

He loaded up the truck, more than ready to head for home. The day hadn't gone as planned, and they lost one of the calves. It happened occasionally, but it always upset him when it did. It was the downside of the job.

Unfortunately, he was also behind a day on appointments, with no end in sight. Even the call with the graduate student from Dallas University looking for a residency hadn't turned out well. The guy had practical experience the intern was lacking, but he had zero personality. And definitely not the laid-back country boy style needed in small-town Tumbleweed County.

His phone rang. Seth Dillinger's name lit up the screen. "Hey, there, what's up?" Joe asked.

"You still out and about?" Seth asked, his question most unusual.

"Headed home now," Joe said, surprised at how good the words sounded. Was it because he had someone to go home to?

"I got a surprise for that young lady of yours. Stop by and see what you think on your way by here."

"Sure thing. Delia loves surprises." Seth didn't live far from the house, so he was an easy drop in. Joe turned onto his driveway and then up to the white ranch-style house. Seth came down the steps of the porch, holding up a tiny long-haired Himalayan kitten.

Joe shook his head. Strawberry Rhubarb pie or Peach Pie perhaps, but a kitten? *No way.* He slid out of the truck. "This is more than a surprise." Joe chuckled.

"Maybe. But it's the last kitten, and I heard from Roger how taken she was with the cats at his place. She's old enough to have a pet of her own. Teach the young'un responsibility." The old man stroked the kitten behind the ears as he cradled it against his chest.

Seth was right. Joe wasn't sure what Marissa would say, but common sense went out the window. Suddenly, he wanted to get his daughter something nice. Something that would make her happy and remind her of him when she went back to Dallas and to keep her company until he could get the legal affairs settled. "You know, you might be right. I'll take her."

"Great. Hold her for a second." Seth held the kitten out. "I've put together a box with some food and litter to get you through a few days. You can let me know how it works out."

Joe took the kitten, cradling it and rubbing her belly. "Will do. And thanks for thinking of us. It really is a great idea." Joe would deal with Marissa and hope she came around to see things his way. Otherwise, he would own a kitten. Not exactly the dog he wanted for the past few years, but never had time for. So much depended on the results of the paternity test, but he was honest enough with himself to realize the kitten would be good for Delia either way.

Joe pulled into the driveway, pleased to see Marissa sitting on the front porch, Delia by her side. It made him think of a mother and daughter sitting together pouring over a book. It was a settling image...like home.

"Good afternoon, ladies," Joe said, drawing near.

"What do you have behind your back, Joe?" Marissa asked, a wide grin on her face.

"A surprise for Delia."

"Me? Yay, I love surprises." Delia hopped down from the chair and ran to meet him. "What is it?"

He pulled his hand from around his back. "A kitten. Seth thought of you and called me. It was the last one available. I agreed with him that you were old enough to have a pet of your own. You must promise to take care of the kitten though," he added.

"Oh, I love it," she said, carefully taking the kitten from his hand and snuggling it against her chest.

"What's her name?" Delia asked.

"Seeing as she's going to be your pet, you get to name her. That's part of the fun."

Delia's smile was a heartwarming sight. "Cool. *Hmmm*, I'd like to call her Sky because her eyes are so blue."

"Great name," Marissa said, joining them, her voice a little crisp.

Delia didn't need to be a part of this discussion, as he fully expected to get an earful. "Run along and play with your kitten while I talk to your aunt."

"I have the prettiest kitten in the whole wide world," Delia beamed.

"She is a sweetheart," Marissa said, though her smile didn't reach her eyes. Delia moved off to play with her new friend.

"Joe, you can't give her a kitten," Marissa said, her voice flat and direct.

"Why not?"

"Because when we go back to our apartment, we can't have a cat. It's called a no-pet policy, and you should have asked me first."

That was something he hadn't thought about. "Then don't leave. Why don't you stay here in Crossroads Creek?" he said before thinking over his response. Though honestly, it wasn't a bad idea. They were all settling in nicely together, so why did it have to change?

"Have you lost your mind?"

"What's back in Dallas that's not here...besides me...and the kitten? You're writing again, you said so yourself. And I heard an active keyboard in the wee hours of the morning." He couldn't believe he was trying to convince Marissa to stay longer, but for his daughter's sake, it was important to him. More than he realized until this very moment.

Marissa shook her head. "Be serious."

"I am. We work well together. We finally figured out how to balance our jobs, but more importantly, we are both getting to spend time with Delia. It'll give me more time to get to know her. I just got my daughter in my life, and I don't want to lose her anytime soon."

"*Shhh.*" Marissa said, pressing a finger to her lips as she scanned the area to check on Delia's whereabouts.

"We can't stay. I need to stick to the two-week plan we agreed on. No more. Delia has school starting soon."

Joe didn't want to press the issue too hard. There was already the future custody looming between them and he didn't want to upset Marissa before he understood exactly what his plans were. "I didn't think of that. I guess the cat will stay with me and Delia will see her when she visits." At least until they knew the future and what it held for all of them.

Marissa frowned. "This isn't fair. You know she's going to be mad at me. Why do I have to be the bad guy? Like I said, you should have talked to me first," she said, hands on hips and watching Delia cuddle her new kitten.

"That's not what I was hoping for. It really was just trying to give her a pet of her own.

You said she's been through a lot and just starting to smile. I really thought it was a great idea," Joe added.

"She seems happy, and she needs a friend. I suppose I could talk to the rental agency and find out the pet fee for a cat. Not that I need more expenses...but to be honest, you might be right. The kitten might be perfect for Delia." The tension visibly melted from Marissa's shoulder and neck muscles, and there was even a hint of a smile.

Joe nodded. The two of them agreeing with each other was the start of co-parenting, if it came to that. "Thanks. It would seem I might have done something right in your eyes. That means a lot to me."

Marissa looked up in surprise. "What do you mean? You do a lot right. In fact, whenever I think about it, I realize you're a natural at being a dad."

It was his turn to be surprised. "Now that's a heavy compliment I can live with. Do you think about me often?" he asked, moving closer.

"No. Yes. I mean, how can I not? If we are going to be closely paired for the next eleven years, we need to be a team."

"I see." It was disappointing she only thought of him in terms of shared parenting, while he was beginning to think of her differently, in spite of the fact she was Molly's sister.

With dinner over and cleaned up, Marissa and Delia took the kitten out on the porch. While Delia played with the kitten, she watched from the porch swing, enjoying the evening as dusk drew near. The door swung open, and Joe joined her.

The promise of a starlit night and full moon had her basking in the glow of the setting sun. It was her favorite time of day, and she was spending it with people she loved. Or in Joe's case, someone she liked a lot.

"I have something to talk to you about, and I'm hoping you can help me," Marissa said.

Joe turned to face her. "What's up? You know I'll do anything, seeing as you've been most kind, sticking around here and working with me while I get things squared away."

"It's about Delia," she said, lowering her voice.

"Let's hear it."

"It's her birthday the day after tomorrow. Laura and I were going to take her to dinner and the zoo, but now that's all changed. I'd like to make the day special for her and need your help."

"I'd love to. We could take her to a farm with animals she can pet, maybe rent some blow-up slides or a bouncy house. Or take her over to Fontana. I think there's a carnival going on there. I could order her a cake."

"Whoa, slow down, cowboy. We don't need anything over the top. I was thinking about decorating your house, maybe setting up a horseback ride, and a special dinner. And I'll make the gluten-free cake since *both* of you can't have gluten." Ever since she found out about Joe having Celiac disease she couldn't help but tease him every chance she got. More and more, the signs all pointed to the fact Delia was his daughter...even if he hadn't admitted to himself just yet.

"Oh. Sorry. This will be her first birthday, or more like my first birthday with Delia. I can't help but be excited. This must be special," Joe said, his eyes lit up like a kid at Christmas.

"I understand." Marissa laughed, her heart melting for the big galoot. Delia was a lucky girl to have him as her father. "Do you think you can help with a modified version?"

"Absolutely. I can stop by the five and dime store and pick up decorations. I need to get her a gift. What would you recommend for her? I don't have a clue."

He was an odd combination of confidence, yet laced with concern and indecision, when it came to his daughter. It bode well for his future as a parent. "The cat was a great idea, so I reckon you'll figure something out. You know she's into soccer, riding, and her cat.

Great place to start." Although at some point, he would need to realize you couldn't buy a child's love and you couldn't always be their friend. Sometimes, the parenting thing would get in the way, and you had to say no.

"Okay, thanks. We can invite Trevor, her new friend, so there's someone her own age here. What do you think?"

"I think it's a wonderful idea. We can have a backyard birthday party, complete with lots of pizza, chicken wings and a veggie tray," Marissa said, settling back in the swing. Delia was totally enraptured with her kitten and was oblivious to their conversation. "Can I ask you something?"

"Sure thing," Joe said.

"Once the results are back from the paternity test and you find out I was right and you're Delia's father, what are you thinking in terms of the future?" she asked, lowering her voice.

"I'm working on it, but first things first, we need the results."

Marissa considered his answer a brush off, deftly skirting the question. She wasn't letting him off the hook that easily. "Surely you've thought this through more than simply playing the waiting game."

"I have. That's why I'm resolved to hire a vet to help me. I know it won't be easy, but like I said, I've missed seven years. Having a daughter would be an answer to my prayers, and any changes or hardships that come of it will be worth every minute."

His impassioned response moved Marissa to tears. She brushed them away before they fell, hoping Joe wouldn't notice. "Will you get married again?"

"Are you offering yourself for the position of wife?" Joe teased.

"Hardly. You and I both know that's impossible, given the situation."

"Is that the only reason?" Joe pressed, taking her hand.

"N...no." Marissa swallowed hard, unsure what else to say. "But I think it's enough of a reason."

"What else, though?"

"My past. I didn't tell you because I didn't want to bring up terrible memories for you, but I had a cheating boyfriend. Molly and Chris were a lot alike. Only Chris took things further and tried to ruin my career when he didn't get his way. I sort of had to start over."

"I'm sorry, I didn't realize. What a jerk. You're a special lady with an enormous heart. Just look what you've done for Delia...and for me. I know it's not been easy for you here, but you stayed anyway. Any man would be lucky to have you in his life."

Anyone except him, she clarified in her head. "Thank you." She wouldn't let it go to her head but couldn't prevent it from going to her heart.

"So, what did you mean, sort of ruined?" he asked, not letting go of her comment.

"It's a long story." And not one she wanted to tell, regardless of the situation. "Let's just say, he trashed my writing, made up stories about me, and all to make himself look better to others. The worst kind of betrayal." It was the final straw in the decision to write under a pen name so that no one could ever betray or hurt her that way again. "So will you marry again?" she repeated the question, wanting to take the focus off her.

"Not without love."

"But you would do it again?" Marissa asked, surprised.

"I used to think I wouldn't, but things have changed. Life has a way of doing that."

"I see." Somehow the thought brought her no comfort, though the warmth of his hand made up for any lack of what she imagined the future would look like. For now, she was here...with Joe.

They sat that way for a few minutes, the silence magnified by the darkness that had set in around them. Unfortunately, duty called, and she needed to rejoin the real world of parenting.

"It's time for me to get Delia to bed. Thanks for such an amazing evening. We couldn't have had a more wonderful sunset," she said, withdrawing her hand and standing up.

"You're welcome. And for the record, I think it's the company that made it spectacular." Joe shot her a wink and grinned.

The man sure had a way with words.

"Thank you." She didn't dare touch the comment much more than that, or she'd start hoping perhaps he really did like her. And not just for Delia's sake.

"Don't forget to dress comfortably tomor row....and wear your boots. We might get a little dirty when we make the rounds." Joe chuckled.

"Is that your way of trying to get me to change my mind about going?" she asked.

"Not at all. Just a warning."

"I appreciate the heads up. Thank you. Delia, honey, you need to wash up and it's time for you and your kitten to go to bed," Marissa said, moving toward the front door.

"Do I have to?" Delia questioned.

"Yes. You need to mind your aunt," Joe chimed in, shocking Marissa.

"Okay. And thanks for the kitten so much, Joe. I love her so much," Delia said, stopping to drop a kiss on his cheek.

"You're welcome, sweetheart." Joe watched his daughter go inside, an interesting expression on his face, but not one she could read.

Marissa would give anything to know what he really thought of the situation. And so far, he hadn't said one word about the paternity test. Was he bonding with Delia and the results didn't matter? It was a love she hadn't reckoned on, and perhaps if the results were in, Delia's birthday would be the perfect time to tell her the good news. She had a feeling Delia would be over the moon.

Jane Doolittle was a lucky woman, and Marissa was more than a little jealous of the heroine in her story. Whether David or Joe, it was all the same.

Joe was one of the good guys.

Chapter Thirteen

♥

"GOOD MORNING. YOU WERE up early. Tap, tap, tapping away," Joe said when Marissa came into the kitchen, looking bright and beautiful, even in her ratty clothes, as she liked to call them.

"I figured I needed to get some words down on the page if I was going with you this morning. Hopefully, you don't have any emergencies get in the way. After that, I thought I would pick Delia up from Wade's place and take her to lunch."

"Sounds like a fun-filled day. All except the working with me part," he teased. "I have it on good authority that I'm a hard boss to please." He'd been looking forward to spending the day with Marissa and Delia, but then Delia got an invitation that held more appeal. What seven-year-old didn't want to hang with a nine-year-old boy and play soccer?

Marissa grinned. "Except I'm looking for more action than playing with cats and dogs."

"Be careful what you wish for." Joe held up the coffee pot to refill her mug.

"I was already in here earlier, and this is my second cup. Just a fair warning. I'll be bouncing off the walls, especially how strong you make it," she teased.

Delia came into the kitchen, fully dressed. "Is it time to go yet? I don't want to be late." She had her soccer ball and cleats in hand, fully prepared.

It would seem his daughter had a crush on Trevor. "Almost. You need to eat some breakfast first."

"Yes, sir. What's cooking?"

Joe moved to the stove and removed the lid from the skillet. "I made you a gluten-free pancake. A Mickey Mouse pancake. Regular ones for your aunt." He shot Marissa a wink.

"Oh, I've never had those before," Delia said, dropping her stuff in a corner and sitting down at the table.

Joe added chocolate chips for the eyes and a whipped cream smiling mouth to the pancake before handing it to Delia. "Here you go."

"Thanks. This looks awesome. Wait till I tell Trevor," Delia said, cutting into one ear, her eyes glowing.

"Would you like a pancake, Marissa?" Joe put one on a plate and held it out to her.

"If you're sure there's enough. I should have come out and helped you cook, but I was using the wee hours of the morning to write."

Joe nodded. "It's all good. I don't cook much, but I can make a mean pancake."

Marissa took the plate and then poured on the maple syrup.

"How can pancakes be mean? My Mickey Mouse is smiling...not mean," Delia said, frowning up at them.

Joe laughed and sat down to join them for breakfast. "It's just an expression that means wicked good."

Delia's brow lines deepened as she pondered his comment.

"He means it's really good," Marissa offered, jumping in to clarify. "And I concur, they are delicious."

"Oh, I get it. It is mean then, for sure." Delia laughed.

Joe grinned, shooting a look of gratitude at Marissa. "I'm glad you both are enjoying them."

"Next time I want a Mickey Mouse," Marissa teased.

"You're on." Joe was pleased she was even thinking there would be a next time. Perhaps there was hope he might convince her to stay longer after all.

Thirty minutes later, they dropped Delia off at Trevor's house and headed to his first appointment.

"So, what's on the agenda?" Marissa asked.

"This morning's visit is for running blood tests on some pigs to test for various levels of contamination. It's part of the FDA regulations to keep food safe for human consumption. I take random samplings, mark them with the proper identification so we know where it came from, and then stop by one of the field labs to drop them off."

"Sounds like a good thing. What else happens?"

"Nothing." Joe laughed. "Not everything is an emergency or exciting. And believe me, routine care and testing helps balance the crazy side of this business. We pay close attention to the results because it helps identify disease, or we try to promote antimicrobial practices amongst the farmers. There is a growing concern about human resistance to medicines and we are trying to circumvent that from happening. It's a balancing act."

"I'll take your word for it, but I'm hoping for something a little more exciting. Sorry," Marissa said, rolling her eyes.

"The second appointment might be a little more to your liking. We are doing fertility checks on some horses, and we need to do an ultrasound on one of the pregnant mares. It's always a highlight to see a foal growing within the mare. Much like a doctor and his pregnant patient when they check for a heartbeat and watch the baby move."

"Now that sounds right up my alley. So I'll get to watch?"

"Absolutely." Joe chuckled. "I'll even let you hold the wand."

"Cool."

Joe grinned. "Now you sound like Delia." He drove to the first farm, grabbing his medical bag and the testing kit from the bed of the truck.

"There's Paul Bennington," he said, pointing toward the man coming to greet them. "This will take me about an hour. What do you want to do?"

"Do you think Paul will mind if I walk around and absorb the sights and sounds of the farm? Maybe check out some animals." "I doubt it. Just don't get into any trouble."

"I'm not Delia," she teased.

"You sounded like her earlier." Joe shot her a wink. "Morning, Paul. This is Marissa Johnson. She's visiting from Dallas. Any issue with her checking out your farm as part of research for a fiction novel she's writing?"

"Good morning. Don't bother me none. What kind of books do you write?" Paul asked.

"Sweet romance," Marissa said, smiling as she shook hands with him.

"If you need any ideas, you just talk to me. I'm always thinking I should write a book, not romance, mind you. Good solid mystery. Yep, one day. A farm is a great place for a setting. You know, like mysterious things happening in the barn. Or animals gone missing. Or—"

"Whoa, Paul," Joe said, holding up his hand. "I've got work to do, and you need to be with me. Some other time on the stories."

Marissa shot him a look of gratitude. "Those are great ideas and I will keep them in mind."

"You do that," Paul said, grinning like she'd just handed him first prize for the fattest pig at the fair. "And let me know if you need anything. The missus can get you some tea if you get thirsty. Betsy would love company. We love it when Joe comes around. Gives us someone to talk to seeing as we don't get out much. Times are tough right now."

"Paul," Joe said, gently reminding the older man they had business to attend. Conversation was always part of the personal visits you made as a large animal vet, but some folks talked more and longer than others. Paul being one of them if you let him.

An hour later, Joe discovered Marissa talking with Becky and sipping tea on the front porch. The two women seemed to have a lot to discuss. Either that or Marissa was going to kill him once they left.

"Hate to break up the party, but we need to go, Marissa."

"Okay. We had such a lovely talk. I hope to see you again, Betsy. Take good care of yourself and get that swelling down in your feet."

"Thank you. Joe, she's a lovely girl. You ought to think about sweeping her off her feet and getting her to stick around."

"Yes, ma'am. I'll see what I can do, but Marissa's got a mind of her own. She would probably prefer a city slicker to some rough around the edges cowboy like me." Joe chuckled.

"I'm right here, and I'm not interested in either. Thank you very much. I prefer to remain single, by choice," Marissa said, shaking her head, clearly vexed by the direction the conversation had taken.

"Thanks for stopping by, Joe," Paul said.

"I'll let you know the results when I get them." Joe tipped his hat toward Becky. "Good day."

"Bye, everyone," Marissa said, following Joe back to the truck.

"Did she talk your ear off?" Joe asked once they were on their way to the next appointment.

"Yes, but it was sweet. Maybe not all the problems with her feet, but she was genuinely nice."

"Don't say I didn't warn you. This job isn't glamorous, just rewarding."

"Well, I for one, can't wait for the next appointment. Definitely swoon worthy stuff. The hero and heroine working together to save the foal."

"I didn't say there was anything wrong with the foal. It's a routine check."

"Maybe so, but that's where reality ends and fiction takes over."

"Well, okay then. Just don't hint to Mary Beth there's something wrong with the foal. She'll be beside herself with worry for the next few months."

"My lips are sealed," she said, zipping a finger across her lips.

It took about ten minutes to get to the ranch across town. It was interesting to listen to Marissa talk about some of the fun things she'd seen and done along the way for her writing. All of his experiences came from day-to-day living, whereas hers were from a sense of creativity and enjoyment of life that pushed her to discover new and interesting things to write about. All in a day's work, but hers sounded more exciting.

Joe introduced Mary Beth and Marissa, and from there, the two started to chat. Non-stop. Women always seemed to have it easy when it came to making friends. Not so much with him. Clients were his friends. Of course, then there was Perry. But he started out as his boss, and then his partner. Not quite the same thing.

"We need to get a move on ladies," Joe said, when he'd heard enough of the mutual admiration society in full speed ahead motion.

"Of course. You know what to do, and Marissa and I can go inside for tea. It's so nice to have someone visit," Mary Beth said.

"Ummm, sorry, Mary Beth. Actually, I really wanted to help Joe with this appointment. I'm doing research for a story that features a vet."

"Oh, I see. Go for it, girl. With the story and the vet," Mary Beth teased.

Marissa flushed a bright pink, knowing full well what she meant. "It's not like that. We're...*ummm*...friends," she said, for the lack of a better word.

"If you say so. Go have fun." Mary Beth waved and headed back into the house, leaving them to do the job he'd come for.

"Ready?" he asked.

"Absolutely. This will be something so different. I want to soak it in so I can write the details."

"It's not exactly romantic, but let's go."

"Not everything has to be romance, but it helps." Marissa laughed.

Joe moved to the stall where Felicity's Fancy was kept. He led the horse out to the main area and tied her lead to the post. It would give him more room to maneuver as he tried to get an excellent picture on the screen. "This is the gel I rub on her belly; it helps the recording device move freely against her coat. It doesn't hurt her at all. Probably feels good, truth be told."

"If I were pregnant, I would like belly rubs too." Marissa grinned.

"Well, okay then," Joe said, suddenly uncomfortable. Mares he could handle the discussion, pregnant women...that was way out of his comfort zone. He attached the cord to the device and turned it on, testing that everything was working.

"Hey, Felicity girl," Joe said, rubbing the mare's nose and her sides gently as he spoke to her, trying to calm her before he started the ultrasound. "Are you going to let me look at your foal?" The horse nudged his hand.

"I can't believe what I'm seeing. You talk to the horses, and they answer. Does this happen often?" Marissa asked.

"It does. Animal care is about communication. It doesn't always work out and their way of talking to you might be a swift kick to the leg, but it helps."

Joe moved the wand over her belly and watched and listened on the recording device for the shape of the foal and for a heartbeat. When he heard it, he motioned for Marissa to come close. He placed the wand in her hand, and covered her hand with his, moving in slow motion to find the heartbeat again.

"There. Listen closely and you can hear the beating heart. And see this here," he said, pointing to the odd shape on the screen. "That's the foal. All four legs and growing nicely. The heartbeat is good."

Marissa listened, not saying a word. Joe could feel her sense of wonder as they moved the wand around. She turned to him, her eyes glistening with tears. "How lovely. Thank you for sharing such a magical moment with me."

"My pleasure," Joe said, realizing he meant every word. They stayed that way for a few seconds before he realized Felicity was nudging him, wondering what was happening. "Your foal is doing great. Nice job, Felicity. All is well," he said, moving to stand next to the mare.

Marissa hugged the mare, surprising him. "You have a sweet baby, Felicity. You're a lucky girl."

"Technically, it's a foal, not a baby."

"I'm not the doctor and I don't need to be technical. Besides, Felicity knows what I mean. She's lucky either way."

Marissa's comment was another surprise. Had she always wanted children of her own and things never worked out as planned? It was a side of her he hadn't known. She was amazing with Delia, but he never considered she might have wanted children once upon a time.

Just like him.

It was soon time to leave, and they said their goodbyes to Mary Beth. Joe dropped Marissa back at the ranch. She was going to pick up Delia and take her to lunch, while he was forced to make up some of the lost time from yesterday.

Joe couldn't believe how exhilarating it was to have Marissa by his side, working with him. Too bad she wasn't interested in becoming a vet. But if there was a way to keep Delia and Marissa in his life, he was all in. His feelings for Delia had grown enough he wasn't even sure he needed to see the test results. With or without the piece of paper, the girl needed a father figure in her life, and Joe wanted to fill those shoes.

And then there was Marissa. Sweet, beautiful, kind, Marissa. It was crazy to even think about them together...as a couple. Especially considering she was Molly's sister. They had fallen into a comfortable routine, and he was loath to let it slip away. And then there was her comment while they were sitting on the porch swing he hadn't been able to get out of his head. *You and I both know that's impossible, given the situation.* She didn't have a list of reasons, just the one wall that seemed to stand between them. It was enough for him to know she was feeling something for him also, or at least he prayed he was reading her right. Neither one of them had a good relationship history, but perhaps it was possible for both to have learned and grown from the past mistakes, enough so that they could get it right the next time around.

He rather enjoyed the chaos, and coming home to family dinners when he could. Even the games and movies they played were fun. It sure beat the empty house and loneliness he'd come to expect over the years.

By simply cutting down on his visits and cutting out snacks and meals at client's houses, he was home more. Socialization had always been a big thing for him, but he was learning to balance it with being more of a family man.

Joe was almost certain deep down in his heart that Delia was his daughter. And as such, he didn't want Marissa to take her back to Dallas. *At all.* Not even for the time it would take to process his custody suit.

Something he didn't think would sit well with Marissa. But what if he could convince her to stay?

Marissa claimed she didn't want to move to Crossroads Creek, but would she agree if they were a couple and got married?

For Delia's sake.

Mostly. The joy he felt when he spent time with Marissa was all of its own accord. But was it enough?

It was a win/win answer that would allow them both to be with Delia all the time. And give them time to let their feelings continue to grow and overcome the hurdles they faced.

It was the perfect answer.

Chapter Fourteen

♥

After picking up Delia from Trevor's house, Marissa headed for the Golden Spoon diner in town. She'd heard plenty about the peach pie and couldn't resist having a piece before she left town. Delia was over the top, non-stop talking about her new best friend, Trevor, all the way into town.

At least at Delia's age, it was an innocent crush that wouldn't have life-changing results when they lost touch. Though if Joe had his way, it would seem Delia would visit often anyway.

Marissa parked the car, and then headed inside, the overhead bell announcing their presence. The bright red booths and checkered tablecloths were classic country diner and cheerful.

"Hey folks," the server called out in greeting. "I'll be right with you. Just grab a seat anywhere."

Marissa waved to acknowledge she'd heard the woman and pointed to a booth by the front window. "Let's sit over there," she said, letting Delia lead the way. Her niece slid in and picked up the menus from the napkin holder and handed Marissa one.

"Thanks, hon. Any idea what you want?"

"Is this the kid's menu?" she asked, pointing to a small section at the bottom of the back side of the menu.

"It is. Looks like your choices are grilled cheese, pizza, a hot dog, a ham and cheese mini sub, or chicken tenders. Everything comes with fries." A standard kid's menu sure to please any child under the age of ten...except for a kid with Celiac disease.

Delia tapped a finger against her chin. "*Hmmm*. I feel like grilled cheese...and a slice of tomato on it. Can you ask them, Aunt Marissa? Please?"

"Only if they have the right bread."

Delia shrugged. "If not, I guess I'll do the plain hotdog with catsup and mustard."

Marissa grinned. "You don't have to change. I just thought you might like to."

"Joe told me he loves grilled cheese and tomato sandwiches. He's just like me."

Delia's world was turning around Joe, which wasn't a bad thing, considering he was her father. "By all means, honey, get whatever you want."

The server stopped at their table. "I'm Christina. What can I get you all to drink?"

"Sweet tea," they answered in unison.

"Perfect. And do you know what you want to eat?"

"Delia would like a grilled cheese sandwich, but can you add a tomato slice and make it with gluten-free bread, please."

"Of course, sweetie. Sounds yummy to me. In fact, it's one of my personal favs. I keep trying to get Beverly, our owner, to put it on the menu." Her smile was infectious, and Delia beamed under the acknowledgement.

"Yay. Thank you," she remembered to say, making Marissa proud of her niece and her manners.

"And for you?" Christina asked, turning to Marissa.

"I think I'll have the same. Sounds delicious," Marissa said, more than willing to join the Joe fan club. "Oh, and we want to share a piece of the famous peach pie I've been hearing about."

Christina smiled, jotting some notes on her pad. "Perfect. A la mode?"

Marissa nodded. "Sure. Let's go all the way."

"You won't regret it," Christina said before moving off to take care of the next customers who had just sat down.

"I like her. She's super nice," Delia said, unfolding her napkin and placing it across her lap. Something else Marissa had taught her.

"Yes, I agree. Lots of folks in town have been nice." Small town living had its own variety of appeal, and Marissa wondered what it would be like to live in Crossroads Creek. A place where everyone knew your name.

"I love it here, Aunt Marissa. People talk to each other more. Laugh more. I wish we could stay here. And Joe is awesome. He's our friend, right?"

Marissa nodded. "He is our friend, for sure." And so much more, but they had yet to break the news to Delia. Perhaps her birthday would be the right time. Provided, of course, the test results arrived and confirmed Joe was the birth father. But then, a whole new set of problems would begin. She would never keep Joe from seeing Delia, but the question became, how much time would he want?

"So, can we move here?" Delia asked.

Marissa choked on the sip of water she had taken. "It's not that easy. My home is in Dallas, and that's where you go to school." She hadn't anticipated Delia wanting to stay. It begged the question of why? Wasn't her niece happy in Dallas? Or was it simply a case of there were so many fun things going on here that she wanted it to continue?

"But you can work anywhere. And I don't mind changing schools. My friend Trevor said he loves his school."

"We'll talk more about this later," Marissa said as Christina delivered their drinks and food.

"Thank you. This looks delicious," Marissa said, having developed an appetite this morning working with Joe. She would have to think of good reasons they couldn't move to Crossroads Creek, because at the moment, she was fresh out of them.

They finished their lunch and headed back to the house. The peach pie had been divine, and they brought some home for dessert tonight. Delia rushed into the house to get her soccer ball, and Marissa stopped just inside the door. She glanced around the room for the hundredth time, wondering about the owner of the place. There was very little by way of nick knacks or personal items. It was cozy, but not quaint.

It needed a woman's touch to make it home. It was something the heroine in the story could give Joe...err, David, that is.

Marissa had settled on a photographer heroine. Someone who needed to trust in love and people and find her way back to happiness. The more and more the character developed, the more she knew she'd found the perfect woman for David. Marissa tossed her keys on the table and noticed mail in the front door slot. She picked up the envelope and discovered it was from the Genetic Testing Agency.

The results were in. And just in time for Delia's birthday tomorrow.

Marissa clutched them to her chest, resisting the urge to tear the envelope open and check the results first. They would finally know the truth. She forced herself to drop the envelope on the foyer table, knowing Joe would see it when he came home.

Chapter Fifteen

♥

LAUGHTER COMING FROM THE kitchen warmed Joe's heart. It was a wonderful sound to start the day. And today was a very special day indeed. *Delia's birthday.*

Ever since Joe sent in the sample, he was consumed with waiting for the answer and trying to figure out what it would all mean. And now, the answer was within his reach, but for the life of him, he couldn't open the envelope. After he spotted it on the foyer table, he folded it in half and slid the envelope in his back pocket, knowing Marissa would have seen it as well.

And last night, when he was alone, Joe placed it on the dresser and walked away, though he must have gone back and picked it up a dozen times or more. It was almost as if he were afraid to open the envelope.

Marissa hadn't said a thing last night. Her silence was unnerving, but not for his lack of trying to get a better sense of how she felt about things while they ate dinner. They had talked about the future once they had the results, and they'd agreed on regular visitation, and he'd been fine with Delia starting school in Dallas until everything was legalized for him to have full custody.

And in his heart...Joe already believed he knew the answer to what was inside the envelope. *His prayer for a family had been answered.*

The question remained, however, what came next? The thought of letting Delia return to Dallas at all didn't sit well with Joe. How could he be expected to let his daughter leave when he'd only just met her. Not only that, but what if he was wrong?

If he opened the envelope and Delia wasn't his flesh and blood, Marissa would vanish from his life and take Delia with her. Everything good he had now, and that he'd come to enjoy, would be gone. Leaving him alone. *Again.*

And then there was, after all, Marissa to consider. She was a loving aunt and Delia's current guardian. What happened if he confirmed Delia was his daughter? Joe would seek custody, but Delia had every right to take her back to Dallas until the dust settled on the case and the judge made a ruling. Unless he could convince her to do otherwise.

Eight years was a long time to make up for in missing time with one's daughter, but it was something Joe fully intended to do. He simply had to convince Marissa to stay. It was the best option for everyone.

"Good morning, ladies. And happy birthday to Miss Delia, our special girl for the day," Joe said, joining them in the kitchen and giving Delia a hug.

"Good morning," Marissa chimed in, glancing his way, a questioning look on her face, complete with white frosting on her cheek.

"I'm eight years old today. It's going to be the best birthday ever with you, Aunt Marissa, and Trevor. And he's bringing Sandy, a friend of his, for me to meet. Can you believe it?" Delia's excitement was contagious as she danced around the kitchen, singing happy birthday to me.

Joe chuckled. "Oh, I believe it. There's nothing more special on your birthday than to celebrate it with friends and family." He moved to grab a paper towel and crossed the kitchen to stand next to Marissa.

"What's up?" she asked, her smile fading.

"You've got frosting on your face." Joe grinned. He stepped closer and wiped the white trail off her cheek, ever so gently, savoring the closeness. The citrusy scent she wore was fresh, reminding him of a warm summer evening on a walk through an orange grove.

"Thanks," she said, her cheeks flushed bright pink.

"Did you see the mail I put on the table for you?" she asked, lines of tension creasing her forehead.

"I did. Thanks." He knew what she was asking, but this wasn't the time or place to explain why he wasn't sure he wanted to open it. Joe was still trying to figure it all out in his head, and he didn't want Marissa to leave until he knew where everything stood. With Delia...and with Marissa. Combined with a conversation they had previously, and how they got along so well, he was hoping she'd say yes when he popped the question of her staying.

"And?" she asked.

"We can talk later," he said, going for a non-committal answer to delay the inevitable.

"Cake looks great, but *ummm*, what is it? No offense."

"It's a Twister board. Delia's favorite game." *Which meant nothing to him.*

"It's where you spin the dial, and it tells you whether to place a hand or a foot on a certain color. Bodies get tangled and twisted, and whoever stays up the longest wins."

"I see." Sounded like a recipe for aches and pains in the morning. "You're a natural when it comes to decorating. Where did you learn to do that?"

"I just look at magazines and follow their leads, though this was fairly simple. I love the creative side of cake decorating."

"That doesn't surprise me, given your entire career is based entirely on your creative abilities."

A fresh flush painted Marissa's cheeks. "Thanks. What a sweet thing to say."

"Simple truth. When is everyone arriving? And what can I do to help get ready? I switched around two appointments just so I could be of help," Joe said, sliding his finger around the edge of the frosting bowl to get a taste.

"Thank you. That's a relief," Marissa said, refocusing her attention on the finishing details of decorating the cake. "You can have the rest of that frosting. I've only got to add the gumdrops for the circles and two Gumby figurines left to do."

"Thanks. This is a treat I never get. And I won't ask what a Gumby is." Joe chuckled.

"This is a Gumby," she said, holding up a green figure. "It bends and twists."

He picked up the bowl and used a spoon to scrape more of the frosting.

"What about me?" Delia asked, stopping next to him. "I want some."

"Grab a spoon. We can share." Joe laughed. "What do you need me to do, Marissa?"

"The homemade pizza needs to get finished first because the dough for the crust needs to rise. You've said you aren't any good in the kitchen, but is it because you actually aren't good at preparing meals, or is it that you don't like to cook?"

"Never really had the time. I'm willing to try if you are right here with instructions, but I make no promises."

"Works for me." Marissa clicked a few buttons on her phone. "After the pizza, I still need to have the decorations hung inside and outside, to set up the table and chairs outside, and move the trashcan closer to the tables. Oh, and hang the piñata," she said, reading off her list.

"Piñata? I don't remember us talking about that?" Joe said.

"We didn't. I saw it in the five and dime when I went shopping for decorations and decided it would be a great addition to the party."

"I love piñatas. And it's a big cow." Delia beamed.

"Of course. What else would Crossroads Creek have had for a piñata?" Joe chuckled. Marissa had far more experience in parenting, another reason he didn't want to lose her. "You would know better than me. Sounds like we better get to work since the birthday girl gets to play," he said, bumping shoulders with Delia.

"Yay. No work for me. What's for breakfast?" Delia asked.

Joe smiled; positive she would want more Mickey Mouse pancakes. "What's your favorite?"

"*Hmmm*. Do you know how to make an egg in a hole?" Delia asked, grinning.

Not at all what he expected. "I'm not even sure what it is to tell you the truth."

Marissa chuckled and continued her artwork for the Twister birthday cake.

Delia giggled. "You really don't know how to cook, do you? Even I know how to make it and I'm only eight."

Joe moved closer and caught Delia around the waist, picking her up and spinning her around, tickling her sides. "Spill the secret, or go without the holy egg," he teased.

"It's egg in a hole, not a holy egg." Delia giggled.

Joe set her down. "Yes, Chef Delia. Please tell me your secret?" he asked, completely serious now.

"If you insist. You butter a piece of bread on both sides. Then cut a hole in the middle with a glass. Put the bread in the frying pan and crack an egg into the hole. Cook it until that side is done, and then flip it. It's easy. My mom used to make them for me, and she never broke the egg."

Joe sucked in a deep breath, unprepared for the reference to Molly. "I see. Well, let's see what I can do to make your birthday wish come true." Delia was just a child and wasn't involved in her mother's poor decision-making abilities, and Joe wouldn't let the memory of what he and Molly shared spoil the day. Especially given that even though he and Molly weren't meant to be together, it would appear they created a uniquely beautiful daughter. For that, he would forgive just about anything in the past.

As it turned out, egg in a hole was rather simple. He made one for Delia and two for him and Marissa. A side of uncured bacon and they were all set. "What do you think?" he asked, holding them out for Delia's inspection.

He laid them on the table in front of her. "This looks so yummy. Thank you, Joe. They're perfect."

Joe's heart swelled a few sizes under his daughter's praise. Marissa had mentioned that if they had the results by today, it might be a wonderful birthday surprise. Would she let him say anything if he didn't open the envelope? Maybe Marissa wouldn't understand his reasoning for holding off, but he hoped she would.

"You did a good job," Marissa said, unable to keep the surprise out of her voice.

"Thank you. I tried. I had great motivation to make it perfect," he said.

Marissa's expression darkened. "Molly?"

"Hardly. Delia. The birthday girl," he added, pointing at his daughter. Maybe he should just open the envelope and get it over with. Tear the band aid off. *Or celebrate.*

"Oh, gotcha. This is good," she concurred.

Delia wolfed down her breakfast. In between bites, she talked non-stop about her plans for the day and the endless fun to be had. "I'm going outside to play. Don't forget, on my pizza I want—"

"Pepperoni, onions, peppers, and tomatoes," Joe said, cutting her off.

"Yup. How did you remember?" Delia asked, stopping by the kitchen door.

"Because it's my favorite also," Joe said, happily pointing out something else they had in common.

"Did you hear that, Aunt Marissa? I'm not the only one who loves tomatoes and all the other good stuff on my pizza."

"I heard, darling. Now run along. We've got to clean up, cook, and get everything ready and only four hours to do it all," Marissa said, shooing her niece out of the kitchen.

They could hear Delia singing happy birthday to herself as she ran down the hall, all too happy to get out of helping with the chores.

The second the front door closed with a bang, Marissa turned to him. "Let's cut to the chase, Joe. You said you got the results. What's the answer? I still firmly believe Molly is telling the truth and I can't wait for you to find out she wasn't all bad. I can't stay any longer than planned, either way so we need to work out the details."

Her tone and attitude were like a one-eighty from when Delia was in the room, taking him by surprise. "Whoa. I'm not the bad guy in all this. And you're right about Molly. I wouldn't have married her in the first place if I hadn't thought she was a good person. Guess I lived too quiet a life for her."

Marissa seemed to consider his words and visibly relaxed. "She always did like to be the life of a party."

"Something I didn't understand until it was too late. I imagine the breakup was inevitable, and I wish I had understood more about love, life, and marriage before rushing into anything. But we have Delia, and that's more than enough reason to recognize the blessing of our marriage, no matter how short."

"So, you're acknowledging she's your daughter?" Marissa asked, though it appeared to be with mixed emotions.

"I am, but I didn't open the envelope. I don't think I need to." It was as though he knew it in his heart, and that was enough for him. Perhaps his desire for a family was overriding common sense.

"You're not making any sense. This is what you've been waiting for." Marissa finished rinsing the breakfast dishes and added them to the dishwasher.

"Because I'm not sure it matters. Let's say I'm her father. Then I want her with me. Let's say I'm not, then I want to see more of her. She still needs a father figure in her life. Why can't it be me? There are enough similarities, and she's a great kid. Lots of people parent children that aren't biological parents."

Marissa turned to him, hands on her hips and shaking her head. "You're serious?"

"Yes."

"You're forgetting one thing. I live in Dallas, and if by any chance Delia isn't your daughter, she will remain living in Dallas with me. Until it's deemed that you're her father, I'm taking her with me when I leave. We can uncomplicate this if you just open the envelope and find out the truth. That way we are dealing in facts."

This is where it got tricky. "I agree, but there is another solution. If I can get you to move to Crossroads Creeks, we all win."

Marissa shook her head. "There's no way I'm moving here. I've already told you that. My life is in Dallas."

"But what if you weren't just getting your own place here. What if you move in with me? It's an answer that works for both of us. The house is big enough for all of us. I'm sure it would be the best solution for Delia, and we can help each other to balance the responsibility of raising a child," Joe said, searching for the right words.

Marissa shook her head. "No. I'm not living with anyone. That would be wrong on so many levels."

"Then marry me." The words were out before he could stop them, and judging by Marissa's expression, she was just as shocked as he was about the proposal. It reeked of desperation, which he wasn't.

Delia was his daughter; he just knew it. The proposal was for Marissa's benefit, but it didn't seem she saw it the same way.

"You can't be serious?"

"I would never joke or tease about something so important to me." He wouldn't back down, because though it was an extreme measure, he felt in his heart it was the right choice.

Joe's work phone rang. Talk about bad timing. This wasn't a good time for an emergency, but then there never was. *This was just the worst*. He turned away to take the call, trying to shift gears and refocus. By the time he hung up, he knew there was no other way available.

"I'm sorry, but I've got to leave. There's an emergency in Wylie, and the vet is asking me for help. I'll be back as soon as I can. I hate leaving you in the lurch on our discussion or preparations for the party, but I don't have a choice." It was times like these that he wished his standards for an employee weren't so high.

"But it's Delia's birthday. Will you be back for the party?" Marissa asked.

"I honestly don't know. I'll send someone over to help take care of setting up outside for you. Maybe Wade can come early. I'll think of something. Please tell Delia I'm sorry."

"She'll be devastated, but I'll do my best to smooth things over. I'm sorry you have to leave, and I will pray all goes well for you and that you're back before you know it."

"Thanks for your understanding. It means a lot to me." Her gaze locked with his, the connection between them riveting. He turned away, knowing he had to leave.

The prognosis for an early return wasn't good based on the emergency call. The fear of bovine flu was serious and a case of all hands-on deck to get the herd vaccinated as quickly as possible. He raced out the door and to his truck, kicking up the dust and gravel as he sped down the driveway.

Chapter Sixteen

♥

Four hours later, Delia's party would have started, but Joe was still working. There were still more cows to be vaccinated, and there was no telling how much longer he'd be here. Sweat dripped off his forehead, and he wiped it with his sleeve. A vehicle pulled into the driveway, pulling up close to the barn.

"Hey, Diana. What's up? I hope you're not having an emergency at your place, as I've got all I can handle here," Joe said, when she moved to stand next to him. Diana had only recently moved to Crossroads Creek where she met Chad Thompson. The two of them were married not long ago and ran a ranch not far from here.

"I heard about the possible bovine flu out-break. I also know how critical it is to get the vaccines going if Mr. Wilson is going to save the herd."

"That's true. Important enough for me to miss my daughter's birthday." Sheer exhaustion let the words slip out, though he didn't want anyone to feel sorry for him. It was his own fault he hadn't made getting an assistant a priority fast enough.

Diana pulled off her cowboy hat and stared at him. "Wait, what? You have a daughter? Since when?"

"About two weeks ago. I'm not scoring any points missing her special day, but what else am I supposed to do? Emergencies come first." This was the only time Joe could remember not liking his job. And this after only two weeks with Delia in his life. Love had a funny way of changing one's perspective, and he had definitely fallen in love with the young girl's sweet personality and outgoing, love-of-life emotional side. A girl after his own heart.

"How old is she?" Diana asked.

"Eight."

"That's a tough age. You really need to get home. I came over to help you, but I think you should let me take over and finish up while you go home and enjoy the party. With your daughter. You only get one chance to get this right, Joe."

Joe shook his head but wanted desperately to say yes. "I can't do that. You're not licensed and have no experience injecting vaccines. I can't afford for anything to go wrong."

"I'm the next best thing to licensed, and I've done vaccinations before. I do them on our herd, as you already know. It's not just to save money...it's because I know what I'm doing." Diana grinned.

"How?" Joe asked, more than a little surprised since she'd never mentioned it before.

"I went to school for large animal science. I intended to finish my last year and become a vet, but life happened, and things changed.

Then I landed in Crossroads Creek and met Chad."

It was as though a ray of sunshine warmed his heart as she spoke. Diana might be the answer to his prayers. God might have brought him to this exact moment in time for a reason. "You've got to be kidding. Why didn't you ever say anything?"

Diana shrugged. "It's not a time of my life I like to talk about, except the meeting Chad part," she grinned. "Besides, I'm busy with my daughter and the dairy farm. I'm happier than I've been in years. So, how about it, Joe? You need to learn to accept help when offered, something I learned the hard way."

"I don't know. What will Randy Wilson think?"

"He'll think whatever you tell him. People around here trust your judgment. Explain to me the system you're using, the dosage you're giving, and then watch me for a few times. Whatever it takes to give you confidence in my ability and then leave," she said, rolling up her sleeves, fully prepared to not take no for an answer.

Joe was more than tempted. Delia was the most important thing in his life, and he needed to make sure she didn't hate him for leaving. It could ruin everything he envisioned for the future. One with her in it. "Go for it. And Diana, not a word about Delia to anyone. I shouldn't have said what I did and there's a lot to still be figured out regarding the entire situation. I can tell you have a way with animals and that goes a long way in my books. Thank you."

"You're welcome."

Joe watched Diana vaccinate five cows, her process flawless. Talking to the animal to relax them. Feeling around the area to check for any internal issues. Alcohol prep. Tapping the needle to remove air bubbles. And finally, the slow injection, so as not to overload the cow's system.

More than satisfied, Joe felt better about leaving. "Nice work, and again, thank you. I'm going to take your advice and get back home. Where I belong."

"Thanks for the vote of confidence," Diana said, moving on to the next cow.

"I'll stop and tell Randy what's going on, and then check in with you later to see how it all went. Call me if you have any issues."

"Sure thing, boss," Diana teased.

Joe waved as he headed for the truck, but then stopped in his tracks and turned back. "Diana, you wouldn't happen to be interested in working for me part-time, would you? Maybe you could get your vet's license. I'll even pay part of the tuition as an employee perk."

"It's nothing I've ever considered. Why me?" Diana asked.

"Because I believe in old-fashioned personal service, and I treat everyone like family. I sense you would be the same way. It's rare to find someone like that these days. Besides, I already know the community loves you." Joe grinned, trying his best to sell Diana on the idea, knowing it was the perfect solution to what he needed to find daily balance in his life.

"I see. I can't say, as I've never regretted missing out on that part of my life because of my husband and daughter. I'd have to talk to Chad and see what he thinks. I think it would be amazing. Especially if we can get a discount on our vet rates." Diana laughed.

Joe nodded and grinned. "Absolutely."

"Can I get back to you on this?" she asked.

"Sure thing. And again, thanks for doing this today. I've got to run, or I'll miss the entire party."

On the way home, the sun came out. It was like a new day as the clouds broke up. Which was exactly the way Joe was feeling. Diana was his first ray of hope that he might have the assistant he needed for work. And just in time to make a commitment to spend more time with his daughter.

Joe made a detour into town, realizing he had forgotten to get Delia a birthday present in all the rush of work and trying to balance being at home. Marissa made parenting look easy, something he hoped to do as well one day as Delia's father.

Thinking of this reminded him he needed to call Rebecca, the local attorney in town.

He googled her number and pressed send.

"Good afternoon, Rebecca Wentworth, attorney at law. How can I help you?"

"Hey, Rebecca. It's Joe Granger. I've got a quick question for you, or at least I hope it's quick because I don't have much time."

"I've got a few minutes. What's up?" she asked.

Joe told her the story of Delia and Marissa's arrival in town. "If I want to gain custody of my daughter, what would I need to do? And how hard will it be?"

"This is a delicate situation. Taking Delia away from Marissa wouldn't be good and a judge might not like it at all, given you haven't been in the picture. Not to mention your full-time job and all the emergency hours required. What would you do for childcare?"

"I'm hoping to convince Marissa to stay in Crossroads Creek. We could work together as co-parents."

"That would be the best solution, but is she willing?" Rebecca asked.

His idea was good in theory, not so much on the reality side. "Not yet, but I asked her to marry me."

"You did what?"

"I asked her to marry me. It's perfect for all of us, don't you agree?" Joe said, hoping for moral support. Not that it would change Marissa's answer, but perhaps give him the confidence needed to push the idea forward.

And?" Rebecca prompted.

"She turned me down," Joe admitted.

"Do you love her?"

Maybe. "We get along great. I'd call us friends with a common interest in Delia." He recalled the moment of connection in the kitchen and wondered if more were possible. Though it did come on the heels of her thinking his suggestion of marriage was preposterous.

"It's no wonder she turned you down. Not real smart, Joe. However, it would be best if you're both on the same page. That being said, you would need proof of paternity. The judge may award you custody if the two of you don't agree because you are her father, but it's not a guarantee by any means. It's always what's in the best interest of the child."

It wasn't the best of news, but at least now he knew what he had to do. Open the envelope. There was no other way. "I understand. Thanks, Rebecca." Joe hung up the phone and ran inside the five and dime for a gift.

The other thing he had to do was convince Marissa to move to Crossroads Creek. He didn't want to lose Delia, but he also didn't want to lose Marissa as a friend. Now, more than ever, he needed her to stay. It's not like he didn't care about her...he did.

Why did it have to be love? What was wrong with mutual admiration and love for Delia?

Chapter Seventeen

♥

MARISSA FELT SORRY FOR Joe that he might miss the party. She knew how important it was to him. Delia had taken the news to heart and seemed a little off from her earlier joy.

Even more mind-boggling was the fact Joe had just asked her to marry him. For all the wrong reasons, of course. It was a lot to wrap her brain around with everything else going on. Which is why she was highly agitated while she made the pizzas, the process much slower going it alone. To make things worse,

Marissa couldn't squash the sting of Joe's marriage proposal. In all her years when she pictured someone asking her to marry them, it was never a matter of convenience. Love was so important and fulfilling for those who found true love. She understood there was never a guarantee, but she would like a fighting chance. To start off knowing a marriage wasn't based on love doomed it to failure.

She was grateful when Wade and Courtney showed up with Trevor earlier than previously arranged. At least everything would be ready in time. The party had started right on time, and Delia seemed placated at the moment since she had Trevor and Sandy to play with. Marissa stepped into the kitchen to refill her iced tea.

She was surprised when Delia suddenly appeared by her side. "When's Joe coming back?" she asked for the tenth time.

"I don't know, honey. It was an emergency call, and he didn't have any choice but to go. There's no one else to help him." She hated making excuses for him, but to be fair, they were real justifiable reasons.

"But he's supposed to be here," she whined, sounding more like a five-year-old than her new eight. It's not like it was a big party, and Joe's absence couldn't be over-looked.

"I tell you what. While the pizza's cooking, why don't we get the grown-ups to play soccer against the kids?" Three on three, and the adults would most likely lose, considering Marissa didn't know the first thing about soccer. Hopefully, she didn't kick the ball and miss and land on her backside. That would be a humiliation she could do without.

Delia shrugged. "Okay. I'm game, especially since you never play soccer with me."

Arm in arm, they headed outside.

"Hey Trevor, want to play a pickup game, us against the grown-ups?" Delia shouted as her friends headed her way.

"Cool, we're in," Trevor said, answering for Sandy as well.

"What a fun idea," Courtney said, as she started stretching. Trevor's mom was lean and fit and looked as though this was going to be a serious challenge. But then she didn't know how under prepared Marissa was at sports. She'd find out soon enough.

"Game on," Wade said, joining in the stretching process. Okay, so with Trevor's parents against the kids, they might stand a chance. These two looked like no strangers to working out and clearly had a competitive nature.

Marissa followed their lead, though the moves were awkward at best.

"Why don't you be our goalie, Marissa? Wade and I will work the field. Maybe between the three of us we can outsmart these kids."

"Works for me." If it was less running...she was in.

Delia and Trevor grabbed a few cones to mark off the field corners and then added a few to mark the goals.

"Are you sure about this, Aunt Marissa?" Delia asked, looking slightly worried.

"No, but for you, birthday girl...anything." Her niece's smile made this endeavor worth the while.

The adults lined up on one side, the kids on the other. Trevor was smart enough to claim first possession since they were younger. Within what seemed like seconds, he kicked the ball to Delia. She maneuvered down the field as Courtney and Wade chased after her. Delia took a long kick at the goal, while Marissa was determined to stop the shot. She moved right to block the ball, just as Delia moved to her right and shot. *And scored.*

"Woohoo! Goal for the kid's team," Delia shouted, high fiving with Trevor and Sandy.

"Don't worry, you'll get it next time, Marissa," Wade said, showing his excellent sportsman and competitive nature.

"Glad you think so. I'll give it a try anyway." They had no idea how terrible she would be at this, and she hadn't counted on the pressure of three kids trying to get the ball past you all at once.

Courtney and Wade moved the ball down the field. Courtney took a shot, but Trevor blocked it. All too soon, the kids were barreling down the field toward her again. Trevor was fast, even moving the ball, his long legs outdistancing his parent's slower pace. He passed the ball to Delia, who then passed it back to Trevor.

Marissa couldn't keep up. Trevor took a shot. Marissa jerked to the right, putting her hands up to stop the ball just as it face planted her, knocking her to the ground. Stars spun lightly around her head as she tried to sit up.

"I'm so sorry, Ms. Johnson," Trevor said, dropping down next to her just as Delia and Sandy arrived on the scene.

"Are you okay, Aunt Marissa?" Delia asked.

Courtney and Wade arrived seconds later.

"I'm fine, I promise. Just rocked my brain a bit. Perhaps I should sit out for a few minutes."

Wade helped her up and over to the porch. "That's what I call giving it your best shot," he teased.

Marissa rolled her eyes at his pun. "Gee, thanks."

"We can still play, right?" Trevor asked.

"Yes, go play. Please don't let me spoil the birthday fun." They all ran back to the field, leaving Marissa alone to watch.

She tried calling Joe, hoping to get an update for Delia, but he didn't answer.

Delia ended up sitting out, letting Trevor and Sandy play to keep it two on two until Marissa could go back in to play.

"Have you heard from Joe?" her niece asked, joining her.

"No. I called, but there was no answer."

Delia scuffed the gravel driveway with her foot. "I should have known he'd miss the party. He's always working. Why do grown-ups work so much?"

Marissa's heart went out to Delia. Life certainly hadn't been going her way lately. She could only pray that any upcoming changes would be well received—and welcomed. "Adults have responsibilities and bills to pay. If people want a nice home, food, clothes, and other things, they must pay for them. Joe included."

Delia didn't seem convinced. "But Joe doesn't have a lot of things. I noticed."

"But Joe does what he does because he loves it, not for the money. He's quite fortunate in that respect." Same as Marissa's choice of career, something they had in common. It was one of the many things she admired about him.

"Meaning he loves being a vet more than he loves being with me?" Delia asked, thinking this through way deeper than Marissa would have thought possible at eight. But then, her niece had always been smart and introspective to the way life was with her mother.

Marissa shook her head. "I didn't say that."

Delia seemed on the verge of crying, and Marissa was at a loss for how to comfort her.

It would seem only Joe showing up could cheer Delia up.

"Why don't you go exploring with the other kids? Remember, we put together a scavenger hunt. It's on the table. I'll put the pizza in the oven, and you'll have about twenty minutes."

"I guess," Delia mumbled, moving off to get the list.

Wade and Courtney came to sit with her, both a little short of breath.

"You okay now?" Courtney asked.

"I'm fine. I just wish Joe would get back. Delia's not taking his absence well."

Wade nodded. "I'm sure he will be if he can. With animals, you can never tell what's going to go right...or wrong in an emergency. Trust Joe and his judgment. He's crazy about Delia, so I know he'd be here if he could."

Crazy about Delia. It would seem it was obvious to more people than just her. And they didn't even know Joe was her father.

An hour later, the pizza was almost gone, and the scavenger hunt finished, after the kids had taken a break to eat. "Delia, honey, it's time to cut the cake."

"But what about Joe?" Delia whined.

"I'm sorry, but we can't wait any longer. We just don't know where he is and when he'll be home," Marissa said, trying to console her niece.

"It's not—"

"Someone's coming down the driveway," Wade said, pointing toward a vehicle headed their way.

"It's him. It's him. Joe's here!" Delia shouted, doing a happy dance.

Joe exited the vehicle, got something from the back seat, and headed their way. Except she couldn't see much of the man behind the giant stuffed animal he was carrying.

"How's my birthday girl?" he asked, grinning at Delia. "This is for you," he said, handing her the oversized stuffed cow.

"I'm great. You came back. You do love me. You do," she exclaimed, reaching for the giant cow. "He's so cute."

Joe shot her a curious gaze before kneeling next to Delia. "Of course, I came back. And yes, I do love you. Never doubt that," he said, his voice solemn.

His answer told Marissa everything she needed to know. Joe had seen the results, and he had the verification needed to know that Delia truly was his daughter. Exactly what Marissa had been trying to tell him all along.

Delia hugged Joe. "I love you too. I think I'll name my cow...Chocolate."

"But the cow is black and white," Joe said, obviously not following the choice, which made two of them.

"But the cow gives me milk and I love chocolate milk the best."

Joe laughed. "Good point. I've got some amazing news for both of you. On the emergency call today, I discovered someone with a passion for animals and healing, and she lives right here in Crossroads Creek. She came to help, and that's why I'm home to spend the rest of your party with you, Delia."

Marissa felt a twinge of jealousy. "She?"

"Yes. *Mrs.* Diana Thompson." He shot Marissa a wink, not missing the reason behind the question. "It's not confirmed, but I'm thinking she and I have reached a deal and there's a good chance she's going to work for me part-time. That will give me more time with the both of you."

Delia danced another happy dance. "Yay. That's the best birthday present ever."

"I'm glad you think so, young lady. Now, how about we go play ball? Marissa, Wade, Courtney, or am I too late?" he asked, glancing around at the adults.

"Perfect timing. We need a rematch after losing to the kids earlier," Courtney said, pulling Wade toward the makeshift field.

"Wait, we were just about to cut the cake," Marissa said, stopping them.

"Sounds like I'm just in time for everything," Joe said, plopping down into a nearby seat.

They sang Happy Birthday and Marissa cut the cake, handing the pieces out one by one.

The kids wolfed theirs down and were off and running in a flash. So much for the time and effort she'd put into making and decorating, but Delia having fun was more important.

Delia rejoined them. "Come on, slow pokes."

Joe put his empty plate on the table. "Coming Marissa?" he asked, eager to join the kids.

"You all go play. Once was enough for me today. Besides, it keeps the teams even."

"She got her brain rattled a little while ago," Delia said.

Joe stopped in his tracks and turned to face her. "Are you okay? Do I need to check you over? Not that I'm a people doctor, but I reckon I can spot injuries."

Marissa flushed, uncomfortable with the sudden attention. "I'm fine. Quit fussing and go play with the kids."

"Well, okay then, if you're sure."

"I'm sure."

Marissa just wanted time to think. If Delia was his daughter, the truth hit her square in the forehead, harder than the ball ever did.

There was no way she could separate father and daughter, but where did that leave her? Alone. Unless she moved to Crossroads Creek for Delia's sake. Give up everything in Dallas, in exchange for Delia's happiness. That's what she needed to remember.

Even if she wanted things to be different with Joe, that ship would never come into port, thanks to her sister. Marissa was under no illusion that Joe would accept anything more than friendship for the sake of Delia.

And she wouldn't marry him without love.

Chapter Eighteen

♥

THE ADULTS LOST. *AGAIN*. The kids were faster and had skills the non-soccer adults couldn't compete against. It was all good though, especially since Joe was eager to run to the bunkhouse for a few minutes. Everything in his future hinged on the results of the paternity test.

"Good game, everyone," Joe said, picking up Delia and carrying her on his shoulders back to the porch.

"Thanks, Joe," Delia said, leaning down to hug him around the neck. "*Ewww*, you're sweaty," she added.

Courtney and Trevor laughed. "We've got to get going, but we had such a good time. I promised to have Sandy home by six," Courtney said.

"*Awww*, do you have to leave?" Delia pouted as Joe lowered her to the ground when they reached the porch.

"We do, kiddo. Sorry," Wade chimed in.

"We'll see you at school, Delia. Nice job playing soccer today," Trevor said.

"Thanks. It was loads of fun. Did you like the scavenger hunt? That was my idea," Delia said, skipping next to her friend as they walked toward the car.

"Yup. Haven't done one before," Trevor said.

"Thanks for coming and sharing Delia's special day," Marissa said.

Sandy stopped at the car and stepped forward to hug the birthday girl "It was nice meeting you."

"Thanks. I liked meeting you too," Delia beamed.

"Glad I could get back and spend some time with everyone. I'm sure Delia had a special birthday because of you all. Thanks for chipping in when I had to high tail it out of here."

"No problem. Glad to help," Wade said. They loaded into the car, and within seconds, all that was left was the dusty trail down the driveway marking their exit.

"Did you have fun, sweetheart?" Marissa asked.

"Yes. The other kids loved your cake. Thank you," Delia said.

"Let's clean up a bit and head inside, where we can reheat some pizza for dinner. Tonight might be a good game night," Joe said.

"Sounds like a plan," Marissa agreed.

"Can we play Twister?" Delia asked.

"Of course. I've just got to run to the bunkhouse and change my shirt. Be right back," Joe added, knowing what he really wanted to do was open the envelope. He'd done well to hold off this long, but no more.

Joe headed for the bunkhouse. After changing his shirt, he stopped at the dresser and picked up the envelope. He knew without a doubt she was his daughter in his heart. Between her eye coloring, the Celiac disease, and their food preferences, it all added up. But until he faced the results on the sheet of paper, nothing was final. *Please, Lord. Let this be the answer I've been praying for.*

His hands shook as he slid open the envelope with his finger.

After all he'd been through, the truth was, he was worried about Marissa once he had the proof and moved forward with his custody suit. There was no guarantee he would win, but there was Marissa to consider in all this. He cared about her. A lot. And taking Delia away wasn't ideal, especially given Marissa was such a large part of Delia's life.

Common sense said it was all wrong to even think of starting a family with Marissa, given his previous marriage to her sister. Joe wasn't looking for love, but a great friend wasn't so bad. Someone to talk to, and to share the day with, someone to laugh and share fun times as Delia grew into a lovely young woman. Except Marissa had already turned him down to move to Crossroads Creek, live together, or marry him.

It was three strikes, and he was out. But then he should have known better. She'd been through her own painful past and wasn't looking for a repeat. They were a lot alike in that perspective. And if it turned out he was wrong about Delia, what then? Wouldn't it be better if he and Marissa were a team? Co-parenting and raising Delia together. Joe could still adopt her, and they could be a family.

He unfolded the letter and scanned the contents. Delia Johnson was a ninety-nine percent match as his daughter. *Daughter.*

Joe had a daughter. *For real.* His heart raced as he ran a hand through his hair. Overcome with joy, he did a fist pump, waving the results in the air. Joe had known in his heart he loved Delia before he opened the letter, how much more so now knowing she was truly his daughter. Family.

At the five and dime, he'd not only bought a giant stuffed cow for Delia, but on a whim, also bought a necklace. *Just in case.* A heart-shaped locket on a pendant that had *Daughter* written on the outside and *Love You Forever* on the inside. His instincts paid off, as this would be the best way he could think of to tell his daughter about him and how he felt. Joe prayed Delia would be just as thrilled with the turn of events as he was about the situation.

He headed back for the main house, his steps double time. Marissa was carrying in another load of decorations. "It's not supposed to rain. Let's leave everything until tomorrow and I'll get up early and take care of it. Tonight's all about Delia and some family time."

Marissa shot him an odd look before glancing at her niece. "Okay, works for me."

"Can we watch my new movie? Aunt Marissa got me Dr. Doolittle...you know, the movie about the doctor who talks to animals?" Delia asked, still bouncing off the walls with the excitement of the day. She was like the Energizer Bunny whose batteries never wore out.

"Of course. That sounds like a great way to tamp down your energy levels," Marissa said.

They heated the pizza and sat down at the dining table. Joe's silence became more than noticeable as the minutes passed. "What's going on, Joe? You seem a bit out of sorts," Marissa asked.

"I am out of sorts, but in a good way." He chuckled. "I've got a special announcement to make, and it concerns the birthday girl."

"Me? What is it? My own pony?" Delia asked.

He hadn't even known a horse was on her list of wants, but hopefully she would consider his gift of more importance. "Not quite."

"Joe..." Marissa said, shaking her head.

Except Marissa was the one who told him that if the results were in, it would make an excellent gift for Delia. He agreed. Her hesitation would only be because of the changes in store with such a pronouncement.

Joe reached into his pocket and pulled out a small gift box, handing it to his daughter.

Delia grinned. "Another gift? Yay." She tore off the paper and opened the black velvet box, peering at the heart-shaped pendant. "Daughter. Why does it say..." she looked up at Joe in confusion.

Marissa gasped, but to her credit didn't chime in to ruin his moment.

"Open the locket, sweetheart," Joe said, coming around the table to stand next to her.

Delia opened it. "Love you forever," she read it out loud and then looked up at him. "Does this mean you want to adopt me? Don't you have to marry my aunt first?"

"No. I don't have to adopt you because you *are* my daughter. The daughter I never knew I had. I hope in time that you will come to accept me as your father."

"I don't understand," Delia said, trying hard to make sense of what she was hearing.

"It's true, honey," Marissa said, reaching across the table to take Delia's hand in her own. "Joe was married to your mom. After they divorced, it turned out your mom was pregnant with you, and she decided not to tell Joe that he was going to be a father."

Joe admired the way she delivered the news, and that she was stepping in to tell Delia what she needed to hear in order to understand.

"Wow. Maybe that's why we have so much in common. I've never had a dad, so this is pretty cool. I mean, not that you didn't know, but that we know now. I have a dad," she said, a slow smiling growing on her face. "A dad for a birthday present. Wait till I tell the kids at school." Delia jumped up to hug him. "Best birthday gift ever."

"I'm so happy you're okay with this. I've wanted family forever, and now I have you," Joe said, unable to keep the tears from forming. He brushed them away as they slid down his cheeks. *Emotional moment times a thousand.* If this is what it felt like to be a father, he was all in and looking forward to many more happy moments like these through the years.

He glanced at Marissa, watching her struggle with the news and Delia's reaction. His heart ached for her, but there was nothing he could do to ease emotional upheaval.

Joe wanted a real family...one that included Marissa, and not just for Delia. It was something he started to suspect but was afraid to delve into too deeply given their situation. Being around Marissa made him feel alive again in a way he never knew would be possible.

Chapter Nineteen

♥

"IT'S BEEN A LONG day, and you need to go to bed, Delia," Marissa said, as the credits rolled at the end of the movie.

"But I'm older now," she whined.

"Yes, you are. And we'll discuss bedtimes in the coming days, but for now, you're tired and you need some sleep. You're supposed to go with Joe to his appointments tomorrow."

"Okayyyy," Delia said, covering her yawn. "I can't wait to tell everyone I have a dad. Can Joe tuck me in?"

Marissa pulled back, shocked at the request. Her heart was heavy, but she refused to give into the jealous feelings threatening to steal her peace. Talk about adding insult to her already bruised emotions.

"Maybe we can both tuck you in," Joe suggested.

"Okay, I like that," Delia agreed, covering a yawn.

"You go ahead, Joe. I'll give you some special time with your daughter and then I'll check in on her after.

"Thank you. That's very sweet of you," he said, watching her, a thoughtful expression on his face.

Ten minutes later, Joe walked back into the room. "Your turn. The birthday girl is so tired she can barely keep her eyes open."

"Okay. I'll make it quick." Marissa made sure Delia was tucked in for the night and lights out. Her niece was exhausted but wanted to stay up and talk about her birthday and check out her presents. And, of course, she was snuggled up tight with her new oversized stuffed cow, with one hand wrapped around the pendant on her neck.

"Good night, Delia. I'm glad you had a lovely day."

"Thanks, Aunt Marissa. It was the best. I still can't believe I have a dad."

"You certainly do, honey. I'm so happy for both of you."

"Did you know? Is that why you brought me here?" Delia asked when Marissa flipped off the light.

"I suspected based on some things I discovered in your mom's stuff. And yes, I wanted you to meet him."

"Thank you. This is the coolest thing ever."

"Sweet dreams," Marissa said, closing the door. Her niece hadn't been overjoyed at the party until Joe showed back up at the house. There was no denying the bond the two shared.

Marissa made her way down the hall to the living room, grateful to be off her feet after such a long day.

"I'm glad you came back here," Joe said, startling her from where he sat in the room's corner. He got up and made his way to the chair closest to her.

"Oh, I didn't know you were still here. What's up?" she asked, aiming for a nonchalant attitude she was far from feeling.

"Earlier, our conversation was interrupted, and I would like to finish it."

"Joe, I don't think—"

"Why can't we get married? Now that we know for sure, it really is the perfect solution. We can share parenting and help each other along the way. It's ideal for Delia to have both the people she loves most in her life."

"I agree, but it's not possible. When I was growing up, I dreamed of ever after and a wonderful man sweeping me off my feet. Never did I picture marrying someone out of convenience. I know people do it all the time, but not me. I've had enough heartache in relationships to steer clear of any more disastrous decisions."

"So, you're a romance writer who doesn't believe in love?"

"I never said I didn't believe in love. I do. But this isn't love. This would be something else entirely and therefore would be classified as a happily ever ends. What I do trust is that God will show me the right person at the right time. Circumventing that would be a terrible mistake. I'm sorry."

"But it's the best solution," Joe insisted, trying to convince her but unsure how to admit the feelings he was beginning to have for her.

"This is to make life easier with Delia. That's not love," she said, her hands nervously twisting together.

"Then you leave me no other choice but to move forward with my plans," Joe said, his heart heavy.

Marissa drew back. "What do you mean?"

Joe stood and moved to the window. There was only one way to break the news. "I'm not letting Delia leave to go back to Dallas."

Marissa glared at him. "I'm her guardian and you can't stop me."

"Maybe not, but I'm working on it. Surely you understand things have changed. I've missed eight years, and I don't want to lose another day. I've asked my attorney to proceed with custody arrangements with Delia. She's my daughter, a child I never knew about, might I remind you? I'm trying to get a temporary injunction to keep her here. I was hoping it wouldn't come to this though. I want us to work together. You're important to Delia and I don't want that to change."

She shook her head, tension rippling from every pore of her body. "You can't do that. I love her. I'm the only solid person in her life. I'm the one who practically raised Delia from the time she was born." Her heart felt ready to explode as she rocked back and forth in the seat, trying to control her breathing.

This wasn't the way things were supposed to happen.

"It's hard to explain, but the knowing part only magnified the feeling of love I have for Delia. I plan to set it up for you to have full visitation, and of course, any time you want to visit, you can. You will always be welcome here."

"But you said we would set up a visitation schedule for her to visit you once the legalities were in place. I can't believe you would do this."

"No, what I said was that we would set up a visitation schedule. It was for her to visit you. Surely you never expected I would have it any other way?"

"I did. I thought you understood. Oh, why did I ever bring Delia here?" she said, her voice bordering on desperation, but she didn't care. This hurt too much.

Joe moved closer. "Because you knew it was the right thing to do and you're a good person with a huge heart and a love for God that wouldn't allow you to do anything else."

"This isn't fair," Marissa said, her eyes glazed over with tears that spilled down her cheeks.

He knelt next to her and took her hand. "Life never is. I'm sorry, Marissa. Just marry me. It's the perfect solution."

Marissa shook her head, pulling her hand from his and brushing away her tears. "I don't want a marriage to be a solution."

"I'm sorry that's your answer, but my offer stands if you decide differently. You can still move to Crossroads Creek, or move in with us, or marry me. Your job allows you to do any of these things and we all win. We would be like a proper family. For Delia. And you and I get along great...and maybe in time..."

"Maybe in time what?" she snapped, latching onto anger to deal with the pain of losing Delia.

"Maybe in time you would come to love me, and I could love you. That we would become a real couple."

It was the first time he even used the word love. Too little, too late. Not to mention it wasn't that he loved her, just a maybe someday. Talk about a slap in the face. "Doubtful. You're not the man I thought you were. Now, more than ever, it makes sense I leave first thing in the morning. I won't fight you in court as that would only hurt my niece. I will trust that you will plan for her to visit me in Dallas."

"Marissa, there's no rush. Stay. Please. We have fun together..." Joe said, the urgency in his voice making her pause.

It wasn't that she didn't want to be here. She suspected that she might have been falling in love with Joe these past weeks, but where did that leave her if he never loved her? Alone in a loveless marriage. Thanks, but no thanks. Everything was different now and the sooner she got used to being alone again, the quicker she would recover. If she ever did... "I finished the rough draft and emailed it to my editor this morning. There's nothing left for me here. I'll make up some excuse to Delia about why I've got to leave in the morning. Then I'll be on my way, as I can't write under these circumstances."

Marissa's heart was breaking, but she wouldn't let Joe see her cry.

Chapter Twenty

♥

J OE SPENT A SLEEPLESS night, upset that Marissa was leaving and there didn't seem to be anything he could do to change her mind. He was also worried how Delia would react to the news her aunt was returning to Dallas.

He couldn't believe she wouldn't even consider his marriage proposal, or even simply move to Crossroads Creek. Marissa was an amazing woman with a heart of gold, and the thought of separating Delia from her aunt didn't set well with him. But what was he supposed to do? There didn't seem to be any other answers.

Throughout the night, the angst stayed with him, his gut telling him this wasn't supposed to be the way things ended. What stung even more was her determination to leave at once, as though she couldn't stand to be around him anymore. Whereas he rather enjoyed her company.

With Molly, it had always been social parties and doing what she wanted to do. Marissa seemed to enjoy just being together, even helping him work. Like they were partners. So why the rush to leave?

"Good morning, Delia," Joe said, spotting her at the table and Marissa at the sink.

Marissa spun around, her eyes bright red, proof she'd been crying. His heart felt as though it was carrying an anchor around it.

"Good morning," they both said in unison, though Marissa's was muffled.

"Morning, Marissa. Is there any coffee left?" he asked, seeing there was, but trying to find something to break the chill between them.

"Yes. I'll pour you some," she offered, filling a cup and handing it to him. Marissa stepped back as though needing to distance herself.

He'd been a fool to think she cared about him. For Marissa, this had always been about Delia. And now that events were unfolding that she hadn't expected, she was bowing up on him. The effect was like that of a door slamming shut in his face.

For the hundredth time in the last twenty-four hours, he wished Marissa would accept his proposal. Couldn't the romance writer, just this once, go for less than happily ever after? Joe sat down at the table, hoping Marissa would follow suit. Seconds passed before she joined him, her hands nervously twisting around the mug as though it were a lifeline.

Joe nodded in her direction, the awkward silence deafening. It was time for Marissa to explain to Delia what was happening, and for them to deal with the fallout.

Marissa cleared her throat. "Delia, honey, I've decided to go back to Dallas since I finished the rough draft. I have so much to do, and Laura has been arranging some events now that my writer's block has lifted and there's a book to release all too soon. Lots of publicity stuff," she explained, glossing over all the real reasons for her sudden departure.

"But I'm not ready to go back, Aunt Marissa. I like it here," Delia said, looking at Joe and then her aunt, as though sensing something was wrong.

Joe reached for Delia's hand. "Trust me, sunshine. I'm not ready for you to leave either and I'm hoping you'll stay here with me. Of course, if you're not happy about the idea and want to return to Dallas with your aunt, I'm sure we can work something out. Maybe then you can start spending more time in Crossroads Creek and eventually transition to your new school here while you get used to the changes." It wasn't what he planned on offering, but somehow it felt right. Causing Marissa pain when all she had done was help, wasn't the answer. And soon, Delia would be with him full-time. This would be an adjustment period for everyone.

Marissa shot him a surprised look, and something else. A hint of admiration, perhaps? "Thank you, Joe. That means the world to me to hear you offer a solution that would make us all happy...at least for now," she added, her voice soft and trembling.

"But I don't want to go to Dallas. I want to stay here with my dad. You can stay here, Aunt Marissa. Just like we are now. It would be awesome. And I can go to school with Trevor and Sandy. Please, Aunt Marissa. Say yes, so that we can stay," Delia pleaded.

Marissa shook her head. "I can't, sweetie. I've got too much going on back in Dallas. If you want to stay with your dad and see how things go, I'm all for it. I want you to be happy."

"But I'll miss you," Delia whined.

Marissa patted her hand. "I'll miss you too. But like Joe, *ummm*, your dad said, we'll work it out to visit together often. I promise. I'll only be a few hours away."

"Well, okay then. I would like to stay here. I hope that doesn't hurt your feelings, Aunt Marissa. I love you so much, but I'd like to try school here with Trevor and Sandy. And I really want to get to know my dad."

Joe felt bad for Marissa, but it did his heart good to hear his daughter wanted to stay with him. "Then it's settled, and Marissa, anytime you want to visit or call, there's a place for you here. Open-door policy."

"Thank you. I'm already packed. I need to go over the rough draft with my editor so I can get started on the rewrite and fill in any holes to the plot she picks up on. I'll be quite busy for the next few weeks, so perhaps this is all for the best." Marissa brushed her eyes with the back of her hand, most likely to keep Delia from seeing her tears.

"I understand. I'll get your things and put them in the car while you and Delia chat." Joe drained off his coffee and stood to leave.

"Thank you," Marissa said, shooting him the hint of a smile, though he could tell it cost her.

Joe headed down the hall and picked up the two suitcases, putting them in her car. Marissa's publicity comment had him confused, but this morning's discussion didn't lend itself to questioning what she meant. Emotions were running high, and he'd wait for a more suitable moment.

Delia and Marissa met him on the porch, the two in a tearful embrace as they said their farewells.

"Thanks for bringing my daughter into my life. I can never repay you, but you will have my eternal gratitude," Joe said, stepping forward to hug Marissa. Her citrusy fragrance wafted around him as he held on for a few seconds longer than necessary.

"You're welcome." Marissa stepped back, her gaze locking with his.

There was so much Joe wanted to tell her, but before he could gather his thoughts, she stepped off the porch, waved. The next thing he knew, her car was kicking up the dust as she drove down the driveway.

"I'm going to miss Aunt Marissa," Delia said, her voice cracking.

Joe pulled his daughter close to his side to hug her. "I'll miss her too." Marissa's departure was real...and wrong. He knew it in his heart the second her car disappeared out of view. But it would seem there was nothing he could do to change her mind.

"Do you love her?" Delia asked, surprising him with her intuitive question.

That was the crux of the matter, and Joe was almost positive he knew the answer. But how did one really know? He messed up love the first time around, so what made him think he could do any better a second time? Why, oh why, did he have to fall for Marissa? That's what made it all so confusing. "I think so."

Delia frowned. "Then why did you let her leave? Grownups can be so weird sometimes."

"Because love takes two people, and your aunt isn't looking for love." Not to mention he was only just figuring it out. "We have to respect your aunt's decision to return to Dallas. It's where she lives, while my life is here."

"Are you happy I'm here?" Delia asked, the doubt in her voice tangible.

Joe kneeled down. "Honey, I'm thrilled beyond words. I've always wanted a son or daughter, and now I have one. And lucky me, no bottles and diapers needed," he added with a grin.

"True. But we should talk about the car I'm going to want," Delia said, wrapping her arms around his neck.

"Let's work on a bike for starters," he offered, unwilling to go down that road just yet. Not for many years, if he had his way.

"Deal."

Joe picked his daughter up. "I love you, Delia."

"I love you too, Dad." The words Joe had wanted to hear from the minute he knew about Delia. Sweet and something he would cherish forever. He just wished it wasn't at Marissa's expense.

The day had gone relatively well, all things considered. Joe took Delia with him to all his appointments, not just the morning ones. With no one to watch Delia, he had to take her with him everywhere. Parenting 101. Don't leave a child alone. When would she be old enough for that? He wished Marissa were here to give him instructions. Suddenly responsible for the sole care of Delia had been unnerving, but he had survived the first day. Delia was now tucked into bed, perhaps later than normal, but she was fast asleep.

Joe moved his things back into his room and then headed down the hall, stopping at the room where Marissa had slept. He pulled the bed sheets off to change and wash them. Her perfume lingered on the pillows, and it made him miss her all that much more. After putting on the new sheets, he glanced around the room. All traces of her living here had vanished, leaving the room void of personal effects.

Off in the corner where she had often sat and typed, he spotted a stack of papers she had evidently left behind in her hasty departure. He crossed the room, curiosity taking hold. Joe was more than a little surprised to see it was the rough draft of her manuscript.

The Cowboy Needs a Wife. Catchy title...for a romance. Joe chuckled.

He flipped through the first few pages and was drawn into the story. Joe sat down on the bed and scanned through the paragraphs. Marissa had promised the book wasn't about him, but this cowboy, no matter what name she used, was Joe. She was about to lay out his private life to the world, and it made him angrier than he'd been in a long time. Truthfully, not since his days with Molly. How could she do this to him? To Delia?

Joe moved to the chair in the corner, flipped on the light, and started back at page one. He had to know what she said if he intended to find a reason to stop this nonsense before it got too far along.

All night long, he read, not stopping. And by the time he was finished, he knew the truth. The story had been about him, but although the woman wasn't a novelist, everything else reminded him of Marissa. Which would have been great, if it weren't for the ending. There was no happily ever after for the couple. The sad truth diffused his anger as quickly as it started. She'd laid out both their hearts and feelings on the page, not just his.

Just a cowboy with a new daughter finding happiness in his new family life. The photographer left him, just like Marissa had done. Her feelings were like an open book as well, and it was obvious she didn't care for him the way he did about her.

Joe was glad he hadn't made a fool of himself and declared his love out loud when he first suspected he had feelings for her. He pulled out his phone and sent Marissa a text, knowing she was most likely fast asleep and would get it in the morning.

Joe: You left your manuscript, and I couldn't resist reading it. Good stuff, except I thought you said you wouldn't write about me. The ending is sad for the couple, but perhaps meant to be. You really have a gift for writing.

Marissa: I can't believe you read it. It's fiction. And it's not you...it's David.

He couldn't believe she responded, which meant she hadn't gone to bed yet. Either that, or she couldn't sleep.

Joe: I thought you wrote happily ever after romance.

Marissa: I do. This one just didn't seem to turn out that way.

Chapter Twenty-One

♥

PULLING OPEN THE BIG double glass doors, Marissa stepped into the marble-tile foyer and made her way to the elevator. Everything about the building spoke of high-end corporate America. She pressed the button for the tenth floor and didn't have to wait long. Her appointment with Laura wasn't for another fifteen minutes, but she hoped to have a little more time with her friend if her schedule allowed.

They'd talked twice since Marissa's return, but mostly, she had spent the time packing up Delia's belongings to ship to Crossroads Creek. She still couldn't process the fact that in her efforts to set right a wrong, she'd lost Delia.

And then there was Joe. Her feelings for him were such a mixed bag of nuts. On the one hand, she really liked him. She may have even been stupid enough to fall in love. But he was Molly's ex-husband. Not to mention, un-requited love was the worst kind. He'd asked her to marry him, but not once had the word love been used.

In the end, Marissa was left alone. All alone. The apartment was far too quiet, and she missed the hustle and bustle of chaos at Joe's place. There was always something going on, and little time to get everything done, but it always seemed to work out. And they'd been like family. Working together and enjoying life.

The elevator bell dinged, announcing her arrival. She made her way down the carpeted hallway, stopping in front of the Sweet Romance Publishing offices. Marissa pulled open the door, stepped inside, and headed for Laura's office. Pausing outside, she waited for her friend to hang up the phone and motion her inside.

"It's about time you climbed out of the rabbit hole you've been hiding in," Laura said, grinning.

"I've been working on the rewrite. You know that's where the story comes to life, and I need the most focus. You should be thrilled," Marissa said, plopping into the seat across from Laura's desk.

"I appreciate the dedication, seeing as you were behind. The partners are pleased to hear we have something from you. Finally. Got me out of the hot seat, so thanks," Laura said, leaning back in her office chair.

Marissa let out a deep sigh. "You were right, the cowboy angle worked. I just needed something that I didn't have to think so hard about for a change."

Laura grinned. "It more than worked, Marissa. It's brilliant."

"I'm glad you like it." The heavy weight of writer's block had truly been lifted off her shoulders.

"Like it? I love it. But...there is one big problem," Laura said, leaning forward in her chair, arms crossed on the desk.

"What's that?"

"Actually, there are two major problems," Laura corrected, shaking her head.

"First, you say it's good and now it's got major problems. Which is it?" Marissa asked, suddenly tense and moving to the edge of her seat.

"This story will never fly with the publisher. Sweet Romance Publishing is dedicated to sweet, clean, and wholesome books, but also happily ever after romances. It's a brand readers can trust. Your ending for the couple isn't a happy one, so it doesn't work and has to be changed."

"But it's the real ending of the story. Sweet romance doesn't mean you always get what you want. And in this case, daddy and the daughter have a happily ever after. What's wrong with that?" Marissa asked, defending her decision to write the story as it happened. Giving it a happy ending just didn't feel right.

"This is fiction, and it matters in the publishing world. People read love stories to escape to a place where love wins the day. You need to rewrite the ending, Marissa. That's not a suggestion," Laura turned on the editor cap and her response was not a choice.

It was rare that their jobs conflicted with their friendship, and this dispute wouldn't change anything between them. Tense...perhaps, for the time being until she finished the book, and it made its way into the world. Maybe then they would laugh about this. "Fine. It won't ring true, but whatever. You're the boss."

"Cut the bull, Marissa. I'm also your friend. So, let's talk about the other major issue."

"Go for it," Marissa said. Whatever it was, it couldn't be as bad as the first.

"The heroine in this book, you realize she's you, right?" Laura asked.

Marissa shook her head and stood, crossing to the window to look out over the cars moving below. "No. Absolutely not. She's a free-lance photographer, someone perfect to capture the essence of the cowboy in his element."

"This free-lance photographer is you, whether or not you want to admit it. You can change the job title and the name, but you can't change the personality or character of the woman in the story. A brother who died, suddenly in charge of a niece, looming deadlines, broken trust in the past. It's you," Laura insisted, unwilling to back down.

Marissa swung around to face her friend. "I—"

"Don't deny it. But here's the deal...Angelina is you and clearly, she's in love with the cowboy. But then, what's not to love? But you didn't write the happily ever after you deserve, and I want to know why?"

Marissa sucked in a deep breath. Was Laura right? Had she been in some blind illusion that Angelina was fictional? "Joe...I mean David, doesn't care for Angelina the way she cares for him. And then there's the sister, I mean brother..."

"Stop with the pretense. You can't even keep it straight in your head, so don't expect to follow the changes. What makes you think Joe doesn't care about you? He asked you to marry him, something you did not tell me, by the way. I'm still mad about that."

"But he wasn't asking because he loved me. He popped the question for Delia's benefit. Think how easy it would be for him if I moved in. He wouldn't have to worry about a thing as a new parent." While she would be madly in love with a husband that didn't love her back. The thought came out of nowhere, shocking her to the core.

"This Joe guy doesn't strike me as someone who would ask you to marry him if he didn't have feelings for you. Besides, why can't it be both?" Laura asked.

"Molly. My sister will always be between us. We can't change the past," Marissa said.

"Molly and Joe were divorced and were only together for a year. You're talking about a lifetime of love if you find the right person. Surely that's what matters. We can't just rule people out because once upon a time, a long time ago, in a far, far galaxy..."

Marissa laughed. Laura's over the top comment shedding light. "You're silly. This isn't Star Wars, it's my life."

"I'm glad we finally got that straight. You need to go after your cowboy and tell him how you feel."

"He already knows. He read the manuscript I left behind and I don't think he's overly thrilled that the main character closely parallels him."

Laura got up and poured a glass of water, handing it to Marissa. "Then he knows the sad ending. Rewrite the ending the way you would want it to happen if you could write your reality ending. The book is crying out for a happily ever after. And when you finish, you need to send the revision to me, but also send it to Joe. Give the man a chance to prove he loves you and that the feelings are mutual. Because honey, from what I'm reading, the man in your story is in love with you."

"*Angelina.* He's in love with Angelina."

"So, you think he loves you, too? What are you waiting for? Love won't wait forever. Go. Write. A. New. Ending."

"But what if he's like all the others? I've had enough of teachers and professors ripping my writing apart and handing out poor grades, and then, of course, there's what Chris did to me to consider. It's not like I can start over again. I've had enough rejection to last a lifetime."

"Except it doesn't matter what anyone says now or in the past. There are always people who won't like your stories or who have ulterior motives with negative comments. You also know how to ignore them. What matters is the readers who love you and...the man who loves you. It's time to trust again."

Marissa nodded, knowing Laura was right. She'd laid it on the line for Joe in the book and it was time she laid it on the line for herself. For them. "I guess that means you don't want to go to lunch."

"Actually, lunch sounds good. Rewrite the ending afterwards." Laura grabbed her purse and headed out the door, leaving Marissa to follow. "And lunch is on you. Call it my Dr. Love bill." Laura's laughter rang throughout the office, causing several employees to turn in her direction.

All the way back to the apartment, Marissa couldn't help but think about Laura's comments. She was right...on all counts. But where did that leave her?

Write the book the way you would really want it to end.

That was living in fantasy land and would only make her heart ache more. The last time she trusted someone with her heart and her life, he trampled over both. It had been a hard lesson, but one that stood her in good stead for the past seven years.

Could she trust her heart and put it all on the line again? And would it be for Delia...or Joe?

The answer hit like a bolt of lightning. She loved them both. *Wholeheartedly.*

Love was worth the risk...at least, that's what she wrote in every book. Why was it so hard to believe that she deserved the same happily ever after kind of love? Joe had asked her to marry him. She replayed the conversation in her head.

Could she trust he would fall in love with her, and not just for Delia's sake? Marissa parked the car and rushed into her apartment, eager to pull up the manuscript and get started. The only way to find out was to put it all on the line and see if he cared about her. Maybe...even loved her.

Just before midnight, Marissa retyped *The End*. More than satisfied, her heart felt lighter than it had in a week. She saved the document and then sent a copy to Laura. Then she pulled out her phone, planning to send a text to Joe. What to say was not a simple thing to decide. She knew she loved him, and that emotion was echoed in the new ending of the story.

Marissa smiled, suddenly knowing what she needed to say...and do.

Tossing her phone on the bed, she turned back to her keyboard. She found Joe's website for the vet clinic and his email address. He mentioned he had read the story and enjoyed it but thought the ending was sad. *Did he also want a different ending?*

Dear Joe,

You were right...the ending of the story was sad. So much so, I've rewritten the ending. I hope you'll reread the last chapter and let me know what you think. I value your opinion above all else. Hope everything is going great at your place.

Love and hugs to Delia.

She hit the backspace to get rid of the last line, instead typing a softer yet inclusive version.

Hugs to you and Delia.

Marissa

P.S. There's a small appreciation party Friday night, 7 PM, at the Sweet Romance Publishing office to celebrate their authors. It's an annual event and I would love both of you to attend.

Marissa attached the file...and then deleted it. She was telling Joe she trusted him with her heart, but there was a better way to show it instead.

Clicking on the file for *The Cowboy Needs a Wife*, and then on the current rewrite version, she pulled up the document and added a title page. One that would include the author's name.

Rose Bloom.

After attaching the new file, she was ready to email it, but paused, her finger poised to hit the send button.

Lord, please, let this be the right decision. Let Joe understand my message and I pray that if we were truly meant to be together, that he feels the same way about me as I do him. And not just for Delia's sake...but for me. For us.

Marissa pressed the send button, encouraged by the lighter feeling in her heart.

Chapter Twenty-Two

♥

IT HAD BEEN A long and busy few days for Joe, but he and Delia were settling into a routine that worked. They both missed Marissa, and Joe toyed with visiting her in Dallas. Delia's question echoed in his head every day. If he loved her, why did he let her go?

He wished there was a better answer than the one he gave Delia. Marissa had been like the warmth of sunshine when she was around. Something was missing, even though the temperatures were still in the seventies.

Joe loved his daughter, but in opening his heart to Delia, he rediscovered the ability to love. And his heart seemed set on Marissa. Tonight, he would broach the subject with Delia and mention a trip to the city, though he was pretty sure she would be thrilled.

Flipping open his laptop, Joe rechecked his schedule for the day. Diana Thompson had done a fantastic job for him with the vaccinations, and after checking with Chad, she was ready to take the test that would allow her to officially work as his vet assistant. She was already handling some of the non-emergency appointments and it had been an immense relief to Joe, and the timing was perfect as he now had more hours in the day to spend with Delia.

A notification dot alerted him to a new email in the inbox. Joe didn't recognize the addressee, and the subject line wasn't much help. *Read this*. Most likely spam. He was ready to send it to the trash, but the opening line grabbed his attention. *You were right; the ending was sad.*

Those were the very words he said to Marissa about her novel. His heart raced as he scrolled to the bottom and discovered the email was from her. Joe scrolled back to the top, eager to read what she sent. He scanned the email, and then read it over twice more, letting the words sink in.

Of course, he would read the new ending and give his opinion. Of course, he would go to the publishing house appreciation party. Of course, he would do anything she asked.

Anything? Anything was a big word.

Would he move to Dallas? The idea came out of nowhere and floored him. Love was powerful, but was it enough to close his business and start over closer to the city?

Joe opened the attachment, and in big bold letters, the title page jumped out at him. *The Cowboy Needs a Wife,* by *Rose Bloom.* He didn't need to read romance to recognize the NY Times bestselling author and the woman some called the queen of romance. Molly used to always have Rose Bloom's books lying around the house.

It would seem Marissa was ghost writing for Rose Bloom. Confidential information she was sharing with him out of the blue. Except the confidentiality clause could only be eradicated by the author. Which could only mean one thing—Marissa was ghost writing for herself. Which, in truth, simply meant writing under a pen name and she didn't want anyone to know. It explained so many of her comments during the time she was here. Had Molly known? Somehow, he doubted it. His ex-wife wasn't the type that could have kept a secret of that magnitude.

Marissa was trusting him with the truth. *But why?*

Joe forwarded to the last chapter and started to read. It only took a few lines before the story came back to him and he found himself immersed in what was happening. When he came to the part where Angelina left, he stopped.

This was the part that hurt deeply. Forcing himself to read on, his interest suddenly intensified. Angelina came back and professed her love, asking the cowboy if he could ever love her...for herself. Not as a mom or an aunt, but for her.

And the cowboy said yes. Emotion swelled in his heart, threatening to spill over. Marissa's message was crystal clear. She loved him and wanted him to know. The next move was his to make.

In her story, David gets the happily ever after he deserves.

In real life, it was the same thing Joe wanted. The answer to his earlier question was just as crystal clear as her message. He would do anything for Marissa, even move to Dallas. He loved Marissa with all his heart, and that meant being partners...fifty-fifty. It would take some doing to find someone to take over the vet business, or perhaps set up a partnership for someone with Diana, but for the sake of love and family...he would do it. Everything about him was wrapped up in Crossroads Creek, except the love of the woman he wanted to spend the rest of his life with.

Joe looked over his schedule and called the vet from the next town over. After securing his permission to be on call this weekend for anything Diana couldn't handle while he was away, Joe planned a trip to Dallas. Friday wouldn't come quick enough for what he wanted.

Marissa.

Chapter Twenty-Three

♥

FRIDAY CAME QUICKLY, BUT not quick enough as far as Joe was concerned. He was anxious to see Marissa again. Delia was equally excited, although she showed her emotions far more than he did. Her non-stop chatter was welcome as it helped calm his nerves.

"Did you tell Aunt Marissa we were coming?"

Joe shook his head. "No. I figured a surprise was in order. Though I talked with her friend Laura at Sweet Romance Publishing, and she assured me it would be okay to arrive unannounced."

"I love surprises. And I really love my new dress. I've never had one so frilly and full. I look like a princess going to a ball. Thank you, Dad," Delia said, the word rolling off her tongue like she'd been saying it for years.

Words Joe would never tire of hearing. "You're welcome, sweetheart. A beautiful dress for a beautiful young lady."

"It's too bad Sarah can't see me in this dress. She has lots of lacy dresses to wear to church," Delia said.

"In time, you'll have a lot of pretty clothes, but always remember it's what's inside a person that counts."

"But I've got blood inside me. Doesn't everyone?"

Joe chuckled. "I'll explain it later. Right now, we've got a party to go to." Joe pulled into the parking garage. After finding a spot on the third floor, they headed for the elevator. To say he wasn't nervous would be a lie. His heart was racing, almost as though they had climbed the stairs to the tenth floor instead of using the elevator.

They exited and headed toward the suite Laura told him to find. He pushed open the door to discover the party was already in full swing.

"Where is she?" Delia asked, pulling him forward.

"I don't know. There are a lot more people here than I expected."

The crowd parted, some moving toward the buffet table, others toward the dance floor. And then Joe spotted Marissa.

He sucked in a deep breath. Beautifully dressed in a peach-colored dress that fell below her ankles in pointed sections, her shoulders left bare, with her short blonde hair tousled with curls to frame her face. *Stunning.*

Joe stepped forward just as her gaze landed on him. Marissa's eyes widened in surprise, her pink glossy lips forming a smile that went straight to his heart. "There she is," he said, pointing in Marissa's direction.

Delia ran forward and hugged her aunt, the two laughing and hugging again. He was witnessing love through a very special window. *A place he wanted to share.*

He stepped forward as they moved toward him.

"You came," she said, her voice low and soft.

"Wouldn't miss it for all the peach pie at the Golden Spoon," he teased.

"Nice." Marissa laughed, her dimples popping with cuteness. "Did you read the ending of the story?"

"I did."

"And..."

Joe had made her wait long enough...for them both. "I loved it. The same way I love you, Marissa. I should have told you before you left. I was afraid you would never feel the same. I don't handle rejection well; in case you hadn't noticed."

Marissa smiled, her eyes twinkling with delight. "I think we both have the same problem."

Delia grabbed his hand and pulled him closer to Marissa. "Will you two just kiss and get it over with? I want to dance."

Joe nodded. "I should probably oblige my daughter's wishes. She gets cranky when I don't."

"I do not. Quit stalling, Dad."

Joe pulled Marissa into his arms. "You can still say no."

"Why would I want to? I wrote the ending, so I know what I want," Marissa said, her voice soft with love.

"You mean, you know what Angelina wants?"

"No. I know what I want, and that's you," Marissa said just as Joe lowered his head, letting his lips softly kiss her cheek before he moved to her mouth, savoring the moment.

"Well, well, what do we have here? I sure hope this is Joe," a buxom brunette said, arms crossed and grinning.

"Miss Laura, did you hear we found my daddy?" Delia asked, jumping up and down.

"I heard. I'm so excited for you, darling," Laura said, hugging Delia close.

"Joe, this is Laura. My editor and best friend," Marissa made the introductions.

"It's nice to finally meet you, considering I've been reading about you in the story. Quite an intriguing man, I must say," Laura said.

Joe found himself at a loss for words. "Thank you, it's nice to meet you too," was all he could muster. The part about the book would take a lot of getting used to, but for Marissa, his life was an open book. At least this once.

"Now can we dance, Dad?" Delia asked, pulling him forward toward the dance floor. "You promised."

"Run along, you two. I'll be right here waiting for you," Marissa said.

"Promise?"

"I promise." The love shining in her eyes was all he needed to see to know today would turn out perfect.

He led Delia to the dance floor for their first father-daughter dance. Holding her hands, he twirled his daughter, bringing her close and then letting her slip away, all while keeping beat to the music. And laughing. "I love you, sweetheart," he said, when the song finished.

"I love you, too, Dad." Arm in arm, they headed back toward Marissa when the song finished.

"Joe, can I talk to you for a minute?" Laura asked.

"Sure thing," he said, hoping she had taken care of his special request.

Marissa eyed them oddly, but he wasn't going to give his surprise away. "Delia, will you keep your aunt busy for a minute? I'll be right back."

"Sure thing. Let's dance," Delia said, dragging Marissa to the dance floor.

Joe followed Laura through one door that led to the kitchen. "Were you able to find what I wanted?"

"Not easy on such short notice, but I found a dozen yellow roses. She opened the cupboard door at the far end of the kitchen and pulled them out.

"These are perfect. Thank you so much. I just need to write the card and then I have a special announcement to make if that's okay with you?"

"I'm guessing you know her pen name?" Laura asked, a hint of surprise in her expression.

"She included it with the revised manuscript."

Laura nodded. "That means she trusts you. Don't hurt her, or you'll have me to deal with."

"Hurt her? I love her. And you'll see how much in a few minutes," Joe said, never more sure of anything in his life.

Joe turned and headed back to the party. He stopped at the deejay's booth, asked for his help, and then headed for Delia and Marissa.

"Ladies and gentlemen, I'm going to pause a moment for a special request. But don't go far. You won't want to miss this announcement or the song that goes with it. It's all yours," the deejay said, sending Joe a thumbs-up signal.

Marissa turned around to where the deejay pointed was pointing at him, her gaze instantly shifting to the flowers he held.

"These are for you. A rose by any other name wouldn't be as beautiful." Joe handed them to Marissa and then reached into his pocket.

"These are gorgeous. I love them," she said, inhaling their sweet fragrance.

"Not nearly as gorgeous as the woman I'm giving them to. Thank you for trusting me with something so important. And in return you should know one of the most important things about me. I love you with all my heart." He dropped to one knee. "I love you enough to know I want to spend the rest of my life with you. Will you marry me, Marissa Johnson, and join Delia and I in a future together as a family?"

Marissa's eyes glistened with tears as she handed the roses to Laura. "Yes. Yes. Yes. I love you both so much, and I've missed you." She launched into his arms, almost knocking him over.

Delia joined in the family hug. "You said yes. I just knew you would. Now I've got a mom and a dad. This is the best day ever."

"Congratulations, you two. Joe, you wouldn't have any single brothers, would you?" Laura asked, hugging Marissa.

"Sorry, not a one. But I know a few good cowboys if that would help," he teased.

"Bring them on." Laura chuckled.

The music started as the deejay cued up This Is Love by King & Country. The song expressed everything in his heart. "May I have this dance, Marissa?"

"You may, now and forever."

Joe kissed Marissa again and led her to the dance floor. He held her tight as the slow song played, making a memory of the moment he never wanted to forget. This was how real love felt, and he liked it. A lot.

"I've thought a lot about the future and we're willing to move to Dallas, if that's what you want. This is a loving partnership, and I aim to make sure you know how much I love you every day," Joe declared.

"I do know, Joe. I can't help but feel the love radiating from you. It's in all you're saying and doing. But I won't ask you to give up your vet practice. I can write from Crossroads Creek or here. It doesn't matter," Marissa said, beaming up at him, her eyes twinkling with love.

"But you said—"

"What I said is that I wouldn't move there just to play house with Delia. I would only move there for love. This is love."

"Are you sure?"

"I'm sure. I've already packed Delia's things. I was going to pay you a visit if you didn't show up tonight. I wasn't letting you slip away without knowing how I felt."

Joe nodded, his heart full of love and peace. "Perhaps we could get you a place to rent in town until we get married. I know most women like long engagements." Talk about a dream coming true.

"I'm not most women."

"You certainly aren't. And that's what I love about you," Joe declared, dropping a kiss on her lips to prove it.

"Don't forget, we have a daughter involved who won't stop bugging us until we are all under one roof."

"True. Perhaps we can talk to her tomorrow and see what she would like most. I'm okay with anything you two ladies decide."

"Good, because I decided I love you and I want to marry you."

"Looks like we agree on a lot more than we suspected. I look forward to the day we become a family." Joe was happier than he ever remembered being in his life. For that matter, it was better than any dream he ever had. This was reality.

"We are already a family," Marissa said, echoing what was in his heart.

Chapter Twenty-Four

♥

THE DECISION HAD BEEN an easy one. Marissa and Delia decided there was no reason to spend months planning and preparing, when all they wanted to do was start their new lives in Crossroads Creek with him.

They were to be married next week at the church by Pastor Phil. Just a small, simple ceremony, Delia wearing her new purple dress.

Today, though, was a special day of its own accord. Wade had given Delia and Marissa the go ahead for their first trail ride, and Joe was taking them on a picnic up to the lake.

The weather was perfect, and the company couldn't have been better.

They arrived at the riding school, both ladies eager for what the day would bring. Joe packed a lunch, complete with sparkling grape juice, to celebrate the momentous occasion.

Wade and Trevor met them at the barn. "Good afternoon. Lovely day for a ride. I've got Trevor saddling up the horses. After I check them over, you're good to go."

"Can I go say hi to him?" Delia asked, always happy to see her friend.

"Sure thing," Joe said, smiling as Delia took off running, very comfortable in her new surroundings.

"You ready for the big day, Marissa?" Wade asked.

"I'm ready for two big days," she said, grinning at Joe.

"Ah, yes. Your first real trail ride and a wedding on the horizon. I'm looking forward to watching the two of you tie the knot. Are you going anywhere on a honeymoon?"

Marissa nodded. "We are just as soon as I finish the book I'm working on. My friend Laura is going to come stay with Delia."

"Tell her to come by the riding school. We can teach another city gal how to ride a horse. You never know, maybe you can convince her to move here." Wade chuckled.

"That would be awesome, but I doubt the publishing house will let her move."

"Don't worry, Marissa. We'll make time to see her and convince her to visit often. Now that Diana's helping, I'm a lot more flexible."

Trevor and Delia approached, leading the horses.

"It's time," Wade said, helping Delia up and into the saddle.

"Yay. I'm so excited and I love Angel. One day, I want a horse of my own."

"In time, Delia." Joe laughed.

He gave Marissa an assist up onto Oatmeal, and then pulled himself up on the thoroughbred they saddled for him. Big Red was plenty large enough to handle his weight and size easily, standing at least seventeen hands high.

"Let's go. Marissa, why don't you take the lead and follow the path? Nice and slow as we get settled in and see how it goes. Delia, if you follow your aunt, I can ride in the back and keep an eye on everything." Joe waited for them to get started and then clicked his heels against the flanks of Big Red, and then, using the reins, followed. Delia was doing a great job, sitting up nice and straight in the saddle, just the way Wade taught her. Marissa set a steady pace and had equally mastered the basics of the walk.

"This is fun. Can we go faster?" Delia called out to him, turning back in her saddle as they rounded a turn.

"Not yet. The path widens just ahead. Let's see how your aunt feels about it."

"Okay," Delia said, disappointment ringing in her voice.

When the path widened, he drew alongside Delia. "Put a little pressure on Angel's flanks and she'll go a little faster and you can pull up next to Marissa."

Delia did as she was instructed and moved to Marissa's right, and Joe fell in on the other side of Delia.

"Are you enjoying the ride? Delia's looking to go faster, and I thought we should discuss it," Joe asked, wanting to include Marissa in any important decisions since they were a team. Not to mention, she was far more experienced in the parenting arena.

"This is a good pace, don't you think? I'm loving the ability to look around and enjoy the beauty. It's so peaceful out here."

"I agree," Joe said, smiling at Marissa over Delia's head, pleased that she understood the special feeling that came from connecting with the great outdoors.

"But I want—"

"Not yet. Let's take this slow. Enjoy God's beauty all around us," Joe said, hoping to stop Delia to keep her from going into a full-blown snit over not getting her way. Stepping up in his parenting role felt right, even if he was giving in to everything Delia wanted.

"But it's boring." She pouted.

"Only if you let it be. Why don't we talk about the wedding, or about the fact that you're starting school the week after?" Joe suggested.

Delia brightened. "I can't wait till the wedding and school. We are going to be a real family, aren't we?"

"We are, honey," Marissa answered, reaching out to lay a hand on Delia's arm.

Her radiant smile was something Joe would never tire of. It was like having his own personal daily dose of sunshine.

"Sandy is going to be in my class, which will be cool. And Trevor promised to play on the playground with me if we get recess together. He doesn't know if the third and fourth graders go out at the same time."

"I'm sure you'll all get plenty of play time together, in and out of school. And we'll have to see about getting you on a soccer team," Joe said, pleased that redirecting Delia's train of thought worked.

"And then one day, I'm going to have a baby brother or sister to play with, right?"

Marissa's surprised expression clued him in that she hadn't even considered that aspect of them getting married for love. Yet. He knew from previous conversations she'd wanted children, and now, the dream could become reality.

"I don't know. We haven't discussed having a baby," Marissa said, a new thoughtful expression setting in.

"But that's what people do when they get married. I mean, you already have me, but a sister or brother would be awesome. That's what I want for Christmas. *Hmmm*, a baby brother and we can name him, *ummm*, David. Like in the Bible. I just learned about him in Sunday school. We would both have the same first letter in our name."

Joe shook his head and laughed. Delia was talking non-stop and not letting the adults get a word in edgewise. "We'll see what we can do, sweetheart. No promises by Christmas, though."

Marissa still hadn't answered, keeping him in the dark about her thoughts on the subject. Whatever she decided was fine by him. He would already have a beautiful wife and daughter. God had blessed him mightily and he wouldn't ask for more.

The path divided up ahead. "Let's take a right here, where the path leads to the river. We can find a spot to stop and have some lunch."

"Can I play in the water?" Delia asked, moving right on to the next subject without missing a beat.

"Let's see what everything looks like when we get there and then we can decide. It should be okay, but we want to be sure," Joe said, not promising anything until he made sure it was safe.

"It'll be good, I just know it," Delia said.

"How do you know that?" Marissa asked, a curious expression on her face.

"Trevor told me, and he knows everything." Delia idolized the boy, though he was only a year older. Given time, he was sure she would realize he was just a boy, especially when Trevor started spending more time with older guy friends when he moved up to the middle school level.

They pulled up to an open area that looked perfect for a picnic. "Let's stop here and tie up the horses." He slid off his horse and then helped Delia down. She ran toward the river's edge. "Don't go in the water yet, young lady," Joe admonished.

"Yes, sir," Delia said, her radiant smile touching his heart.

Marissa had dismounted and led her horse to the tree. "You're good with Delia, and I appreciate that you have no problem stepping in to take the lead. This whole co-parenting thing is rather nice."

"Thank you, that's quite a compliment, Mrs. Soon-To-Be Granger," Joe said, stopping to kiss his future wife. Something he liked to do often.

Marissa's eyes twinkled. "So do you?"

"Do I what?" he asked, confused.

"Do you want a baby?"

Joe sucked in a deep breath. What he wanted was his happily ever after, no matter how that looked. "I want you and Delia. We could have a baby, but only if you think it's right for us as a family."

Marissa's soft sweet smile widened, her eyes glassy with unshed tears. "I never thought I would get the chance. Delia's always been like my daughter, but I would love to have a baby."

"Then it's settled. Baby David by Christmas," Joe teased.

"What if it's a girl?" Marissa laughed at his silliness as they walked hand in hand toward the river.

"Then we'll have to try again for David," Joe said, unable to keep from grinning. He wouldn't mind at all.

Marissa shook her head. "Or how about we name the baby, Deborah, another strong biblical name?"

"We could do both. Just saying."

"I guess we'll leave that up to God," Marissa said as they joined Delia by the river.

"Can I go in?" Delia asked, putting an end to the conversation.

"Yes, but stay right in that area where it's shallower. Take off your boots and socks and roll up your jeans," he said as he headed back down the bank.

"Yes, sir."

"Can I go play in the water too?" Marissa teased.

"You can do anything you want, as long as you take me with you," Joe said, unable to believe the joy that came from loving someone and sharing your life. All of his anger toward Molly had vanished. He could forgive her anything knowing she was the reason Delia and Marissa were in his life.

God's plan for Joe had been there all along. He just hadn't known or understood his dream would come true until Marissa and Delia landed on his porch one crazy day. They not only managed to turn his life upside down, but they turned it right side up...all at the same time.

Epilogue

A YEAR LATER...

Marissa still couldn't believe the changes in their lives. Asking for Delia's input had proven to be a catalyst to move things along. Not only did she want them to get married at once, but she was more than a little pushy about the whole baby sister or brother request. And what Delia wants, it would seem she would get.

What was supposed to have been a small church wedding performed by Pastor Phil turned into a community affair. Everyone wanted to be a part of the newfound joys in the local vet's life. And Diana was more than amazing. With her vet's license on the horizon shortly, Joe had offered her a partnership, and she accepted. She would still be busy on the farm and with her own family, and Joe would be busy with the clinic and his growing family. Not to mention, keeping up with the horses that now filled the barn. Horseback riding had become a favorite family outing, though for the past couple of months, Marissa had stopped riding.

With Diana's help, they even managed to convince Joe to hire an intern. Family and career were finally hitting all the right notes in his balanced life, and they had God to thank for leading them down this path.

And while Joe stayed busy taking care of the animals and his family, Marissa was busy churning out the next book in her series, something high in demand after *The Cowboy Needs a Wife* hit the NYT Bestseller's list.

"So how are you feeling, Mrs. Granger?"

"Like a basketball about to pop," Marissa said, rubbing her well-rounded belly.

"A beautiful basketball. And you still have another month."

"Don't remind me. The babies are active all the time, even when I want to sleep."

Joe kissed her. "Does that help?"

"Always. Takes my mind off everything," Marissa declared.

"Good. Where's Delia?" Joe asked.

"I let her go to Trevor's place. Sandy is joining them, and they are going horseback riding."

"It would seem she has a new interest other than soccer," Joe observed, frowning.

"Yeah, it's called friends. Relax."

"I'm not letting my daughter date until she's eighteen," Joe said.

Marissa laughed. "Good luck playing the dad card when the time comes. Lucky for you, you've got a quite a few years before you need to worry. Perhaps the two of us can come up with a plan. Don't forget, she's only nine. This is just friends hanging out."

"I like the sound of that. At least David and Deborah will have a big sister to guide them. By the time the twins are in their dating teens,

Delia will graduate college and I'm sure be ready to take charge."

"The two of you will be a force to reckon with." Marissa grinned, leaning her head on Joe's shoulder.

"Sounds perfect. Just like my wife."

"I'm not perfect."

"You are for me." Joe kissed her soundly, the same way he did every day to remind her just how much he loved her.

****

If you enjoyed this sweet and charming romance, be sure to check out the **ALSO BY ELSIE DAVIS** section on the next page for more clean and wholesome romance.

Next up – Book 6 – The Life of a Cowboy

Want to keep in touch with new releases and what's happening in the world of Elsie Davis?

Sign up for the monthly newsletter at Elsie Davis.com

The greatest compliment you could give an author is to leave a review in order to help other readers discover the same great stories you enjoyed. Amazon/Bookbub/Goodreads are all great places. Many thanks!!!
Another great way to keep in touch - *Follow Elsie Davis on FaceBook*

Also By Elsie Davis

Sweet, Clean, and Wholesome Stories...with a Happily-Ever-After Guarantee!

Great Smoky Mountain Getaways
(Christian Inspirational – Women's Fiction Romances)
Juliet's Journey to Love
Poppy's Path to Love
Rachel's Road to Love
Taylor's Trek to Love
Grace's Getaway to Love – 2025
Dixie's Detour to Love – 2025
Angel's Adventure to Love – 2025

Crossroads Creek Cowboys
(Christian Inspirational Romances)

The Heart of a Cowboy
The Help of a Cowboy
The Return of a Cowboy
The Care of a Cowboy
The Dream of a Cowboy
The Life of a Cowboy – 2025
The Tears of a Cowboy – 2025

Holidays in Hallbrook
(Sweet Romance Series for Holidays Throughout the Year)

Welcome to Hallbrook, New Hampshire. A small-town filled with the unexpected, lots of love, and of course, a beloved dog to ramp up the excitement.

Love & Order (Labor Day)
Love & Family (Thanksgiving)
Love & Peace (Christmas)

Love & Chocolate (Valentine's Day)
Love & Hope (Mother's Day)
Love & Liberty (Independence Day)
Love & Honor (Veteran's Day)
Love & Joy (Easter)
Love & Adventure (Father's Day)
Lov & Cheer (New Year's Day – TBD)

Sundancer's Legacy

(Contemporary Christian Romance)

Sundancer's Star

Sundancer's Joy
Sundancer's Majesty – 2025

2025/2026
Sundancer's Heart

Sundancer's Miracle
Sundancer's Glory
Sundancer's Kiss
Sundancer's Moon
Sundancer's Splendor

Trinity River Romances
(Sweet Western Romance)
Ranchers and farmers depend on the Trinity River for water, but when a secret conglomerate starts buying up property by fair means or foul, it's time for the landowners of Tumble County to fight back—Texas style. But what they don't count on, is finding love in the process.
Back in the Rancher's Arms
Small Town, Big Secrets
The Firefighter's Miscalculation (2026)
Love Advice for the Cowboy (2026)

Crestfield Inn Romances

If you like special kinds of soulmates, a splash of the supernatural, and wholesome relationships, you'll adore this sweet bit of fun filled with romance and mystery.
Turning Back Time
Turning Up Roses
Turning Down Pie

Celebrity Corgi Romance
(Standalone Sweet Romance/Light Mystery)
If you like light mystery mixed in with your happily-ever-after, you'll enjoy this second-chance romance and the race to save an adorable Corgi.
Digging the Driver

Gold Coast Retrievers
(Standalone Sweet Romance/Light Mystery)

Special Golden Retrievers help their humans solve mysteries, save lives, and even find love...
Defending Dakota

About The Author

Elsie Davis is a *USA Today and International Bestselling Author* of over 30 sweet, clean, and wholesome romances, and a member of the ACFW. She discovered the world of Happily-Ever-After romance at the age of twelve when she began avidly reading Barbara Cartland, the Queen of Romance, and has been hooked ever since. After building her dream log home on top of a small mountain, she turned her attention to do what she loves most, writing. Elsie writes sweet Contemporary Romance and Contemporary Christian Romance from her heart...hoping to share a little love in a big world.

When she's not writing, she can be found birding, kayaking, camping, fishing, playing disc golf, and taking nature walks—hoping to spot wildlife. Basically, she loves all things outdoors, EXCEPT cold weather. She and her husband are avid Caribbean cruisers, but Elsie's favorite vacation was their cruise to Alaska. (In spite of the cold!) Indoors, she enjoys a toasty fire, and of course, a great romance with a guaranteed Happily-Ever-After.

https://www.elsiedavis.com